Dear Readers,

I wrote *The Cinderella Deal* a long, long time ago, but it's still one of my favorites because it was so hard to write and I learned so much writing it. I'd written six romantic comedies before this one and in all the commentary on them, there was one recurring theme: My stories were a little . . . cold. More comedy than romance; no heart, no soul. That was a fair assessment; if there was one thing I'd learned in my creative writing classes it was to avoid melodrama, to never be sentimental, to go for irony and detachment whenever possible, because otherwise I'd get killed in the critiques. But I think I knew all along I was wimping out, that if I'd had any backbone, I'd have gone first for the hearts of my readers, so I decided that for my first book for Bantam, I'd try something new, something different. Hearts would be touched, tears would be shed. By God, I was going to be *emotional*.

Then I sat down to write it and I'm here to tell you, writing comedy may be hard, but writing honest emotion is ten times more difficult. Every time I got near an over-the-top moment, I had to fight my knee-jerk tendency to step back into irony or even worse, to make a joke. After a while it got easier, and I can truthfully say that there are moments in this book that are downright weepers—well, I cried—but the important thing I learned is that tragedy is like comedy. You can't add it to a book, you have to find both the humor and the pain within the story and then write both as truthfully as you can, even if it means that critics will accuse you of being sentimental or melodramatic. Good stories are about both hearts and minds, but the heart always comes first.

Here's hoping you like the heart at the center of *The Cinderella Deal*.

Best wishes,

Jenny Crusie

Jenny Crusie

BANTAM BOOKS BY JENNIFER CRUSIE

The Cinderella Deal
Trust Me on This

JENNIFER CRUSIE

~

The Cinderella Deal

BANTAM BOOKS
NEW YORK

The Cinderella Deal is a work of fiction. Names, characters, places, and incidents are the products of the author's imagination or are used fictitiously. Any resemblance to actual events, locales, or persons, living or dead, is entirely coincidental.

2010 Bantam Books Mass Market Edition

Published in the United States by Bantam Books, an imprint of The Random House Publishing Group, a division of Random House, Inc., New York.

BANTAM BOOKS and the rooster colophon are registered trademarks of Random House, Inc.

Originally published in hardcover in the United States by Bantam Books, an imprint of The Random House Publishing Group, a division of Random House, Inc., in 1996.

ISBN 978-0-553-59336-5

Cover design and illustration: Melody Cassen

Printed in the United States of America

www.bantamdell.com

2 4 6 8 9 7 5 3 1

For Jack Andrew Smith,
a true hero and firefighter,
and the best of all possible brothers

ONE

THE STORM RAGED dark outside, the light in the hallway flickered, and Lincoln Blaise cast a broad shadow over the mailboxes, but it didn't matter. He knew by heart what the card on the box above his said:

> Daisy Flattery
> Apartment 1B
> *Stories Told, Ideas Illminated*
> *Unreal but Not Untrue*

Linc frowned at the card, positive it didn't belong on a mailbox in the dignified old house he shared with three other tenants. That was why he'd rented the apartment in the first place: it had dignity. Linc liked dignity the way he liked calm and control and quiet. It had taken him a long time to get all of those things into his life and into one apartment. Then he'd met his downstairs neighbor.

His frown deepened as he remembered the first time he'd seen Daisy Flattery in the flesh, practically hissing at him as he shooed a cat away from his re-built black Porsche, her dark, frizzy hair crackling around her face like lightning. Later sightings hadn't improved his first impression, and the memory of them didn't improve his mood now. She wore long dresses in electric colors, and since she was tall, they were very long, and she was always scowling at him, her heavy brows drawn together under that dumb blue velvet hat she wore pulled down around her ears even in the summer. She looked like somebody from *Little House on the Prairie* on acid, which was why he usually took care to ignore her.

But now, staring down at the card on her mailbox, appropriately backlit by the apocalyptic storm, he knew there was a possibility he might actually have to get to know her. And it was his own damn fault.

The thought gave him a headache, so he shoved his mail into his jacket pocket and went up the stairs to his apartment and his aspirin.

Downstairs, Daisy Flattery frowned too, and cocked her head to try to catch again the sound she'd heard. It had been something between a creaking door and a cat in trouble. She looked over at Liz to see if she was showing signs of life, but Liz was, as usual, a black velvet blob stretched out on the end table Daisy had rescued from a trash heap two streets over. The cat basked in the warmth from the cracked crystal lamp Daisy had found at Goodwill for a dollar. The three made a lovely picture, light and texture and color, silky fur and smooth wood and warm lamp glow. Unbelievably, fools had thrown away all three; sometimes the blindness of people just amazed Daisy.

"Hello?" The petite blonde across the chipped oak table from Daisy waved her hand. "You there? You have the gooniest look on your face."

"I thought I heard something," Daisy told her best friend. "Never mind. Where was I? Oh, yeah. I'm broke." She shrugged at Julia across from her. "Nothing new."

"Well, you're depressed about it. That's new." Julia took a sugar cookie from the plate in front of her and shoved the rest toward Daisy with one manicured hand, narrowly missing Daisy's stained glass lamp. The lamp was another find: blue, green, and yellow Tiffany pieces with a crack in one that had made it just possible for her to buy it. The crack had been the clincher for Daisy: with the crack, the lamp had a history, a story; it was real. Sort of like her hands, she tried to tell herself as she compared them to Julia's. Blunt, paint-stained, no two nails the same length. Interesting. Real.

Julia, as usual, had missed color and pattern completely and was still on words. "Also, you're the one who has to come up with the bucks for the feline senior cat chow. I should eat so good."

"Right." Daisy scrunched up her face. She hated thinking about money, which was probably why she hadn't had much for the past four years. "Maybe leaving teaching wasn't such a good idea."

Julia straightened so fast, Liz opened an eye again.

"Are you kidding? This *is* new. I can't believe you're doubting yourself." She leaned across the table to stare into Daisy's eyes. "Get a grip. Make some tea to go with these cookies. Tell me a story. Do something weird and unpractical so I'll know you're Daisy Flattery."

"Very funny." Daisy pushed her chair back and went to find tea bags and her beat-up copper teakettle. She was sure the tea bags were in one of the canisters on the shelf, but the kettle could be anywhere. She opened the bottom cupboard and started pawing through the pans, books, and paintbrushes that had somehow taken up housekeeping together.

"I'm not kidding." Julia followed her to the sink. "I've known you for twelve years, and this is the first time I've heard you say you can't do something."

Daisy was so outraged at the thought that she pulled her head out of the cupboard without giving herself enough clearance and smacked herself hard. "Ouch." She rubbed her head through her springy curls. "I'm not saying I can't make it as an artist." Daisy stuck her head back into the cabinet and shoved aside her cookie sheets long enough to find her teakettle and yank it out. "I believe in myself. I just may have moved too fast." She got up and filled the kettle from the faucet.

"Well, it's not like you ever move slow." Julia took down canisters one by one, finally finding the tea in a brown and silver square can. "Why did you put the tea in the can that says 'cocoa'? Never mind. Constant Comment or Earl Grey?"

"Earl Grey." Daisy put the kettle on the stove and turned up the heat. "This is a serious moment, and I need a serious tea."

"Which is why I'm drinking Constant Comment." Julia waggled her long fingers inside the canister and fished out two tea bags. "I have no serious moments."

"Well, pretend you're having one for me." Daisy sighed, envying Julia's optimism. Of course, Julia hadn't quit a safe and solid teaching job to become a painter, or spent the past four years living on her savings until she didn't have any. Daisy felt her head pound. "Julia, I don't think I can do this anymore. I'm tired of scraping to pay my bills, and I'm tired of trying to sell my paintings to people who don't understand what I'm doing, and I'm tired—" She bit her lip. "I'm so tired of worrying about everything." That was the thing, really; she was worn down from the uncertainty. Like water on a rock; that was what the edge of poverty did to you.

"So what are you going to do?" Julia asked, but somewhere there was a faint sound, half screech and half meow, and Daisy cocked her head again instead of answering.

"I swear I hear a cat crying," she told Julia. "Listen. Do you hear anything?"

Julia paused and then shook her head. "Uh-uh. Your water's starting to boil. Maybe that's it."

Daisy took the kettle off while Julia took down two mismatched cups and saucers, plunking her Constant Comment tea bag in a Blue Willow cup and Daisy's Earl Grey in the bright orange Fiestaware. Daisy poured the hot water over the bags and said, "Pretty" as the tea color spread through the cups.

"Forget the pretty tea." Julia picked up her cup and carried it back to the table. "You're in crisis here. You're out of money and you can't sell your paintings. How's the storytelling going?"

"Budget cuts." Daisy sat down across from her with her own cup and saucer. "Most libraries can't afford me, and it's a slow time for bookstores, and forget schools entirely. They all say I'm very popular and they'll use me again as soon as possible, but in the meantime I'm out of luck."

"Okay." Julia crinkled her nose as she thought. "How else were you making money? Oh, the jewelry. What about the jewelry?"

Daisy winced with guilt. "That's selling, but Howard won't give me the money until the end of the month. And he owes me from the end of last month, but he's holding on to that too. It's not that much, about a hundred, but it would help." She knew she should go in and demand her jewelry money, but the thought of Howard sneering at her wasn't appealing. He looked so much like her father that it was like every summer she'd ever spent with him condensed into two minutes.

Julia frowned at her. "So how much do you need? To keep the wolf from the door, I mean."

Daisy sighed. "About a thousand. Last month's rent, this month's rent, and expenses. That would get me to when Howard pays and then maybe something else would turn up." That sounded pathetic, so she took a deep breath and started again. "The thing is, I quit so I could paint, but I'm spending all my time trying to support myself instead of concentrating on my work. I thought I'd have a show by now, but nobody understands what I'm doing. And even though I almost have enough paintings for a show, I'm not sure what I'm doing is right for who am I now anyway."

Julia sipped her tea. "Ouch. Hot. Blow on yours first. What do you mean, you're not sure what you're doing is right? I love your paintings. All those details."

"Well, that's it." Daisy shoved her tea away to lean closer. "I like the details too, but I've done them. I think I need to stretch, to try things that are harder for me, but I can't afford to. I'm building my reputation on primitive narrative paintings; I can't suddenly become an abstract expressionist."

Julia made a face. "*That's* what you want to do?"

"No." Daisy shut her eyes, trying to see the paintings she wanted to do, paintings with the emotions in the brushstrokes instead of in the tiny painted details, thick slashes of paint instead of small, rich dots. "I need to work larger. I need—"

The mewling cry that had teased her earlier came

again, louder. "That is definitely a cat," Daisy said, and went to open the window.

The wind exploded in and stirred Daisy's apartment into even more chaos than usual. Liz rolled to her feet and meowed her annoyance, but Daisy ignored her and leaned out into the storm.

Two bright eyes stared up at her from under the bush beneath her window.

"You stay right there," she told them, and ran for the apartment door.

"Daisy?" Julia called after her, but she let the door bang behind her and ran out into the rain. Whatever it was had vanished, and Daisy got down on her hands and knees in the mud to peer under the bush.

A kitten peered back, soaked and mangy and not at all happy to see her. Daisy reached for it and got clawed for her pains. "I'm rescuing you, dummy," she told it when she'd hauled it out from under the bush and it was squirming against her. "Stop fighting me."

Once inside, she wrapped the soaked little body in a dish towel while Julia and Liz looked at it with equal distaste.

"It looks like a rat," Julia said. "I can't believe it. You rescued a rat."

Liz hissed, and when Daisy toweled the kitten dry, it hissed too.

"It's a calico kitten." Daisy got down on her knees

so she could go eye to eye with the towel-wrapped little animal on the table. "You're okay now."

The mottled kitten glared at her and screeched its
meow with all the melody of a fingernail down a
blackboard.

"Just what you needed. Another mouth to feed,"
Julia said, and the kitten screeched at her too. "And
what a mouth it is." Julia shot a sympathetic look at
Liz. "If you want to come live with me, I understand," she told the cat. "I know you're legally dead,
but even you must draw the line at living with a rat."

Liz glared at the kitten one more time and then
curled up under the light and went back to sleep.

"A kitten doesn't eat much," Daisy said, and went
to get food. She found a can of tuna on the shelf over
the stove, stuck behind her copy of Grimms' fairy
tales, a jar of alizarin crimson acrylic paint, and her
cinnamon. She took down the can and called back to
Julia. "Want some tuna?"

"No. I just came over to bring you the cookies, and
then I got distracted." Julia and the kitten looked at
each other with equal distaste. "You know, this is not
a happy rat."

"Stop it, Julia." Daisy dumped the tuna onto a
china plate covered with violets, scooped a third of it
into a half round of pita bread, and divided the re-
maining two thirds between Liz's red cat dish and a

yellow Fiestaware saucer. She took the dishes back to her round oak table, dropping Liz's red bowl in front of her as she went. Liz was so enthusiastic about the tuna, she sat up. Daisy put the yellow saucer in front of the kitten and stopped to admire the violets on her plate next to the complementary color of the Fiestaware. *Color and contrast,* she thought. *Clash. That's what life is about.*

"Daisy," Julia said. "I know you're going to freak when I say this, but I can loan you a thousand dollars. I want to loan you a thousand dollars. Please."

Daisy froze and then turned to face her friend. Julia stood beside the table in the light from the stained glass lamp, looking fragile and cautious and sympathetic, and Daisy loved her for the offer as much as she was angry that the offer had been made. "No. I can make it."

Julia bit her lip. "Then let me buy a painting. You know how I feel about the Lizzie Borden painting. Let me—"

"Julia, you already own three of my paintings." Daisy turned back to the cat. "Enough charity already."

"It's not charity." Julia's voice was intense. "I bought those paintings because I loved them. And I—"

"No." Daisy picked up the plate with her pita on it. "Want some tuna? I can cut this in half."

"No." Julia sighed. "No, I have papers to grade." She shoved her chair under the table and looked at Daisy regretfully. "If you ever need my help, you know it's there."

"I know." Daisy sat down next to the kitten, trying to concentrate on it instead of on Julia's offer. "If you come across an easy way to make a thousand bucks, let me know."

Julia nodded. "I'll try to remember that." The kitten screeched again, and she retreated to the door. "Teach that cat to shut up, will you? Guthrie is not going to be amused if he finds out you're keeping a cat in his apartment building. The only reason Liz gets by is that she's ninety-eight percent potted plant."

Once Julia had gone, Daisy got down on her knees next to the table so she could look the kitten in the eye. "Look, I know we just met," she told the cat. "But trust me on this, you have to eat. I know you've had a rough childhood, but so did I, and I eat. Besides, from now on you're a Flattery cat. And Flatterys don't quit. Eat the tuna, and you can stay."

Daisy picked up a tiny piece of tuna and held it under the kitten's nose. The kitten licked the tuna and then took it carefully in its mouth.

"See?" Daisy scratched gently behind the kitten's ears. "Poor baby. You're just an orphan of the storm. Little Orphan Annie. But now you're with me."

Little Orphan Annie struggled farther out of the towel and began to eat, slowly at first and then ravenously. Daisy pushed the unruly fuzz of her hair back behind her ears as she watched the kitten, and then she began to eat her pita.

"You're going to have to lie low," she told the kitten. "I'm not allowed to have pets, so we'll have to hide you from the landlord. And from the guy upstairs too. Big dark-haired guy in a suit. No sense of humor. Flares his nostrils a lot. You can't miss him. He kicked Liz once. He looks like he has cats like you for breakfast."

The kitten finished the tuna and licked its chops, its orange and brown fur finally a little drier but still spiky.

"Maybe you're an omen." Daisy stroked her fingers lightly down the kitten's back while it moved on to cleaning the plate. "Maybe this means things will be better. Maybe..."

She began to tell herself the story again, the story of her new life, the one she'd been building for the past four years. She'd given up security to follow her dream, so of course she had to face years of adversity first—four was about right—because without adversity and struggle no story was really a story. Now the next chapter would be her paintings finally selling, and maybe her storytelling career suddenly taking off too. And a prince would be good. Somebody big and warm to keep her company. It had been seven months since Derek had moved out—taking her stereo, the creep—and she was about ready to trust somebody with a Y chromosome again. Not marry anyone, certainly; she'd already seen what that part of the fairy tale could do to women. Look at her mother. The thought of her mother depressed her, but Annie abandoned the empty plate and began to lick the dampness from her fur, and the scratchy sound brought Daisy back to earth.

Forget the prince. Stories were all well and good, but princes weren't stories, they were impossible. Daisy had known that from the time she'd realized that her mother's promises that her father would be back were a bigger fairy tale than anything the Brothers Grimm had ever spun out. Nobody was ever there when you needed someone. *You're born alone and you die alone,* Daisy told herself. *Remember that. Now think of something to get yourself out of this.*

Annie curled up and went to sleep. Liz licked up the last of the tuna and fell unconscious with pleasure. Daisy sat silently for a long time, staring at the patterns in her stained glass lamp.

Upstairs, Linc stretched out on his chrome and black leather couch, bathed in the cool light from his white enameled track lighting, his headache receding but his troubles intact. It didn't help that the mess he was in was his own fault.

He'd lied.

Linc winced. He wasn't a liar; he couldn't ever remember lying before. But he also couldn't remember anything he'd ever wanted as much as he wanted to teach history at quiet, private Prescott College. And he hadn't lied about anything important in his interview for the job: his credentials were all real and impressive, and his goals were honest and good.

Linc closed his eyes. Rationalization. None of that mattered. He'd lied. The memory of his interview came back in painful detail. Dr. Crawford, dean of humanities, and Dr. Booker, head of the history department, had interviewed him. Dr. Crawford looked like a retired southern cop: big, beery, genial, with an overall air of stupidity. He wore a bow tie in what Linc thought of as a feeble attempt at an academic look. Dr. Booker needed no such camouflage. He looked as if the moisture had slowly seeped out of him over the years, leaving only a dried-up little shell behind horn-rimmed glasses. Linc's dreams of a department headship had begun when he saw that Booker was older than God.

And things had gone well at first. They'd been impressed with his credentials, impressed with his first book, published four years before, impressed with his demeanor, and just impressed with him in general. He knew he was good; he'd sacrificed for years to make sure that he was good, that he'd published in the right places and presented at the right conferences, that his background was above reproach, that he always did and said the right thing. And now the only question was, would they think he was good enough? But that hadn't been the question. The question that Dr. Crawford, his fat lips pursing, had asked was "Are you married, Dr. Blaise?"

"No." And then he'd seen the look on Crawford's face: regret. Linc hadn't made it as far as he had in a very competitive profession by being slow. "But I'm engaged," he'd finished. Then he'd had a stroke of what at the time had seemed like genius. "Prescott would be the perfect place for us. We've been waiting to get married until I was established so we could raise our children the old-fashioned way."

Crawford didn't just thaw, he blossomed. "Excellent,

excellent. Old-fashioned values. You'll definitely be hearing from us again, Dr. Blaise."

Dr. Booker had sniffed.

And Linc had wondered if he was losing his mind. It was bad enough that he'd created a fiancée; he'd really sent himself to hell when he'd babbled about mythical children. And the weird part was, it seemed so true while he'd been saying it. Not the fiancée part, but the idea of settling down with some elegant little woman and reproducing in a small town. The pictures had been there in his head, sunny scenes of neat lawns and well-behaved children in well-ironed shorts. *You're pathetic, Blaise,* he'd told himself at the time. *And you lied. God's going to make you pay for that. You'll probably get struck by lightning.*

But as it turned out, it wasn't lightning that slugged him from behind, but Crawford. He'd been invited to speak to the faculty on his research, the standard job-talk audition for a college position. And, Crawford had written, make sure you bring your fiancée.

Right. Linc punished himself with the thought of it and drank more beer. He deserved this. If Prescott wouldn't take him on his own very considerable merits, he should have just let them go. There were other schools. And once he finished the book he was working on—

But he couldn't finish the book. Not at the city

university, where he was now, not while teaching three awful, mind-numbing classes. To finish the book he needed someplace like Prescott. And to get Prescott he needed a plan.

Linc shifted on the couch. He actually had two plans. One was to show up without a fiancée and probably not get the job. That one had the benefit of honesty and not much else. The other was to convince somebody to pose as his fiancée, and then if he got the job, he could tell the people at Prescott that the engagement was off. They couldn't take the appointment back. As a plan it wasn't great, which was why he'd put it out of his mind until three days before the interview, but as the deadline approached, it became more attractive. It beat not getting Prescott.

All he needed was a woman who was reasonably bright and reasonably attractive in a sedate sort of way who was willing to lie through her teeth and then quietly disappear. His first thought had been Julia in the apartment downstairs. They'd had a brief affair and parted friends. She would probably do it, he knew, but she'd make a mess of it. Julia was too sharp-looking and too sharp-tongued. He needed a... a wifely-looking woman. A *Little House on the Prairie* kind of woman. A woman who could lie without batting an eye.

Daisy Flattery.

No, he thought, but logically, she was his best hope. *Stories told,* her card said, so truth was not one of her virtues. And Julia had said she was straight as an arrow, and he trusted Julia's judgment if not her restraint. Daisy Flattery was about six inches shorter than he was, with a round midwestern body; if he put her in one of those old-fashioned flowered dresses, Crawford might go for it. Since she seemed to hate him for some reason, she'd probably have to be in desperate need of money before she'd agree to spend any amount of time with him, but she didn't look rich. Desperation could drive a person to do things he or she would never contemplate ordinarily.

I should know, Linc thought gloomily, and stared at the ceiling. *Make a note to call Julia about the Flattery woman,* he told himself, and then realized that he didn't have time to make notes. It was Tuesday. He was due in Prescott on Friday. He felt dizzy for a moment, and realized it was because he was holding his breath, his response to tension for as far back as he could remember. "Breathe, Blaise," his football coach had yelled at him in high school the first time he'd passed out during a game. "You gotta keep breathing if you want to play the game."

He inhaled sharply through his nose and then stretched out his hand for the phone and punched in Julia's number.

Five minutes later, Linc was listening to Julia laugh herself sick. "You told them what?" she gasped at him when she could talk. "I can't believe it."

"Knock it off," Linc said. "It's not funny. This is my career at stake here."

"And we all know that's more important to you than any of your body parts." Julia snickered. "I love this. You want me to be the little woman? No problem. I'll get one of those dweeby little dresses—"

"*No.*" Linc broke in before Julia could get too attached to the idea. "I need a professional liar, somebody who won't start giggling when the chips are down."

"Daisy." Julia's voice went up a notch in approval. "She's wonderful, absolutely trustworthy."

"Except she tells lies for a living."

"She tells *stories,*" Julia corrected Linc with some heat. "Unreal but not untrue, that's what Daisy says. And anyway, it's not like you're lily-white here, bud. You're the one who created the Little Woman Who Could."

Linc exhaled in frustration.

"I can't believe you lied in the first place," Julia went on. "I would have said it wasn't possible. You really are a stick-in-the-mud, but maybe this will break you out of that rut—"

Linc glared at the phone. "I like my rut. I have to go. Good-bye."

"Because you really are solidifying before my eyes—" Julia said, and he hung up.

Oh, God. He let his head fall back against the leather chair back. Three days and no fiancée. He was in big trouble, and his only hope was a nutcake. There had to be a better way. The last thing he needed was to pin all his hopes for the future on Daisy Flattery.

He got up and got himself another beer.

Daisy spent the next morning trying to drum up work and failing miserably. When she got home, the kitten had escaped and was sitting on the doorstep waiting for her. So was the landlord, a man Julia called Grumpy Guthrie. *Oh, no,* Daisy thought, and then straightened her shoulders and went to save her cat, marching past the dark-haired thug from upstairs who was washing his nasty black car. She disliked his car almost as much as she disliked him; it looked like something Darth Vader would drive.

Guthrie pointed at the kitten as if it were a cockroach. "That's a cat."

"Yes, I know." Daisy took a deep breath and then

smiled at him. Daisy knew she wasn't beautiful, but God had given her something better than beauty—a glowing, wide-mouthed, man-melting smile, courtesy of her mother and a long line of southern belles who'd dazzled their way through history. It was her only physical weapon, but it never failed her. It didn't now.

Guthrie smirked at her.

Behind her she heard the cat kicker turn off the water just in time for Annie to tear out one of her ungodly meows.

Guthrie flinched. "Daisy, you're a month behind on the rent, and you're not allowed to have pets."

"I know." Daisy pumped out more wattage on her smile. "You know I'll pay the rent. I've lived here for eight years, and I've never let you down, have I?"

Guthrie closed his eyes. "No, but the cat—"

"I'm only keeping the cat until its owners get back," Daisy said truthfully, since she was sure Annie's owner would never get back to this apartment house. "It's a very valuable cat, you know." She dropped her voice to make Guthrie a conspirator with her. "One of a kind. An Alizarin Crimson. Very unusual voice. Don't tell anyone, or there'll be catnappers all over the place." Guthrie blinked and she let her voice go back up to its natural register. "I'm sure Julia won't mind, and the people upstairs will never know. It's such a *little* cat."

"But they do know," Guthrie said. "Dr. Blaise knows. He's right here."

Daisy turned to look at the cat kicker. He was as tall and broad and threatening as she'd told Annie, his hair thick and blue-black and his eyes dark and intense. He leaned on the car watching them, and he didn't look angry, he looked calculating.

Daisy went for it. "Do you mind, Dr. Blaise?" She hit him with her smile in the best tradition of her ancestresses.

He blinked. And then he grinned at her. It wasn't the usual feeble smirk that men gave her after she'd blasted them, it was a wide-awake grin. He had a great mouth for a thug. "I don't mind at all, Miss Flattery. It's an honor to have an Alizarin Crimson in the building."

Daisy felt uneasy, but she wasn't about to look a gift jerk in the mouth, even if he did kick cats. "Thank you, Dr. Blaise. That's very sweet of you." She smiled at him again, and his own smile widened.

Strange man.

"I'll have the rent for you soon," she promised Guthrie, and he went off, shaking his head.

Daisy scooped up the kitten and turned to go, but

the cat kicker called her back. "Could I have a word with you, Miss Flattery?"

I knew it, Daisy told herself. *It was too good to be true.* She took a deep breath and turned back, smiling her brains out, prepared to do whatever she had to do to keep Annie from becoming an orphan again.

TWO

HE CAME OUT from around the car, dressed only in black sweats and incredibly old white sneakers. His broad body was beautifully proportioned, but it didn't matter. Daisy knew about proportion from art class, but she knew about men from life. *Yes, he's pretty, but forget it,* she told herself. *He kicks cats. He drives an evil black car. And Julia says he has track lighting.* Definitely not somebody she wanted to spend time with.

Still, she did need to be nice to keep her cat. She hit him with her megawatt smile again. He grinned back, immune. Oh, well. "Thank you so much for saving my kitten, Dr. Blaise. If there's ever anything I can do in return . . ."

"There is. I have a business proposition for you." His smile disappeared. "Strictly business."

Daisy snorted mentally. It would be strictly business. He probably didn't have the imagination to make a pass. Which was a relief, because when she turned him down, he'd probably kick her cat. "Business, Dr. Blaise?"

"Linc." He stepped closer and took her elbow. "Why don't we go in and talk about it?"

Oh, great. He was an elbow taker. A steerer of women. Daisy removed her elbow from his grasp. "How about my place? Herbal tea?"

He closed his eyes, said "Wonderful," and followed her into the house.

Linc stopped inside the apartment door. The place looked as though it had been ransacked. There were drawers open, papers everywhere, lampshades askew, books on the floor, and a huge black cat sprawled out in the middle of the mess, doing an excellent impression of death. Linc waited for Daisy to scream and call the police, but she just dropped the little calico cat into an overstuffed chair full of yarn and clothes and stepped over the black cat to move toward the kitchen.

It must always look like this. How could she stand it?

She pulled her bright blue velvet hat from her head, and her thick hair fell down in tangled little kinks, dark curls with deep glints of red against the bright, bright blue of her loose hip-length sweater. Under the sweater she wore an ankle-length skirt checked in hot rose and electric blue. Linc winced at all the color.

Then she opened the refrigerator and got him a bottle of beer, and her approval rating rose.

He took it gratefully. "No herbal tea?"

Daisy grinned at him, a nice, cheerful grin with none of the dazzle of her earlier beam. "I thought you'd prefer this."

"I do. Do you have an opener?"

Daisy took the bottle back and looked around absently for an opener. Not finding one, she hooked the cap on the edge of the counter and smacked it with her hand to pop it. Then she handed the bottle back.

Linc checked to see if there were glass chips on the top. *Remember, you need her. Be polite.* "That was very efficient. Thank you."

He sat opposite her at the big round oak table. She turned on the stained glass lamp that stood to one side, and it cast a Technicolor kaleidoscope on the wall and ceiling. More color. Everywhere he looked, color and clash. How did she sleep in this place?

"A business proposition." Daisy tilted her head at him. "I'm not a businesswoman."

Linc studied her in the lamplight: masses of dark curls, big dark brown eyes spaced far apart over a blobby nose sprinkled with freckles, a wide, rosy, generous mouth. This woman looked so wholesome, she could sell milk to dairy farmers. If he put her in a real dress instead of clothes three sizes too big for her, she could pass for the girl next door. She wasn't his type—he liked lethally elegant blondes, the tinier the better—but she was definitely Prescott's type. He cheered up considerably.

"I need a favor." Linc leaned forward, exerting all his charm. "A practical, extremely confidential business favor." He saw her draw her eyebrows together at the word "confidential," and added, "It's not illegal. And I'll pay your back rent."

The eyebrows flew up. "That's three hundred dollars."

Linc nodded. "I know. I'm desperate. I need a fiancée for twenty-four hours." That sounded a little odd, so he clarified it. "Only a fiancée. A *platonic* fiancée."

"I understand that you're not propositioning me." Daisy folded her hands on the table like a polite child. "You can stop making that clear."

Linc relaxed a little. "Good." He took a swig of his beer, amazed at how much more difficult this whole thing was than he'd imagined. It wasn't just the embarrassment of admitting what he'd done. It was also Daisy Flattery. There was something about dealing with this woman that reminded him of the way he'd felt messing around with the chemistry set he'd had when he was a kid. Volatile. Unpredictable.

Her voice broke his train of thought. "Why do you need a fiancée?"

He took a deep breath and told her, haltingly at first but then becoming more confident as he explained, and she didn't throw him out or go off into fits of laughter.

"You're in a mess," she agreed when he was finished. "But I don't see how you think I could help you. I'm hardly the wifely type."

"No, but you could be for twenty-four hours. I'll pay for a new dress. All you have to do is pretend to be the wifely type for the space of a speech and a cocktail party. I'll have you out of there by Friday at midnight and back home by Saturday afternoon."

Her laughter spurted, something between a giggle and a snort. "So you pick me up out of the gutter, and I get a new dress, and I pretend to be something I'm not, and then at midnight I run away and turn back into a pumpkin." Her grin widened. "It's a Cinderella story."

"I guess so." Whimsy was not Linc's strong suit.

"And you get the job of your dreams and the time to finish your book." She tilted her head. "I like this story. Everybody wins."

"Even Guthrie," Linc said. "He'll get your back rent."

"And I get to keep Annie." Daisy smiled at him, warm with gratitude. "That was nice of you to tell Guthrie you didn't mind, since you didn't know whether I'd do this or not, and you hate cats."

He looked at her, puzzled. "I don't hate cats."

Daisy's smile cooled. "I saw you kick Liz once."

Linc frowned at her. "Liz?"

Daisy nodded to the black cat curled up among the debris on the floor. It hadn't moved at all since he'd been there. Maybe it was dead. He fought back an urge to poke it with his foot to see if it was breathing, and that brought back his earlier encounter. "Oh, yeah. I didn't kick it, I just nudged it out of the way with my foot. It walked on my car."

Her smile disappeared completely. "The *nerve* of her."

Oh, great. Now she was off on a tangent, mad at him for something he hadn't even done. "Forget the cat. Will you do it?"

She thought about it, setting her jaw, and Linc had a sinking insight into how stubborn she could probably be. Then she said "Yes," nodding sharply. "For a thousand dollars."

Linc jerked back. "A thousand?"

"That's what I need." Daisy smiled at him, the smile that had probably sunk a thousand ships in her lifetime. "I'm not really going to be Cinderella unless you rescue me completely, you know."

When she smiled at him like that, it was hard to think. Imagine what that smile could do in Prescott. *Make a note to have her smile a lot in Prescott,* he told himself, and gave in. "All right. A thousand dollars."

She stuck her hand across the table, and he took it. Her grip was firm and warm. "It's a deal, then," she said. "A Cinderella deal."

"Great," he said through clenched teeth. Just what he needed, a child bride who still believed in fairy tales. "Are you free tomorrow afternoon about one so we can rehearse this story?"

Daisy nodded. "For a thousand dollars, I can be very free."

"Good." He stood up and patted her on the head. "I'll see you tomorrow, then."

Daisy was still glaring at the door when he'd closed it behind him.

A cat kicker. An elbow grabber. A head patter.

"This may be a Cinderella deal," Daisy told the cats, "but trust me, he's no prince."

When Linc picked Daisy up at one, he'd been having qualms all morning, and the sight of her outfit didn't help relieve them. She was swathed in a short-waisted bright yellow eyelet dress that hung down to her ankles and hid completely whatever shape she had, and her hair was mashed under that damn blue velvet hat. Where did she get those huge clothes? She wasn't that little; she had to be five eight at least. She'd look smaller if she stood next to him though. *Make a note to tell Daisy not to stand next to Booker,* he told himself. She'd look like a Valkyrie next to a gnome.

He held the passenger door open for her, and she looked at his car as if it were roadkill.

"What?" he asked her. "What's wrong now?"

"This car is evil," she told him in a thrilling voice. "This car needs an exorcist."

He looked at her dumbfounded. "This car is a Porsche. I rebuilt it myself. This is a *great* car."

"It's black and long and low and it looks like hell on wheels." Daisy shook her head. "I can't believe a college professor would drive something like this."

This wasn't a new thought; everybody who saw the car started from the same place, which was that it wasn't his type of car and how the hell could he afford it. The truth was, Linc had found the car while he'd been working in a scrap yard during grad school and, in a moment of absolute insanity brought on by his disbelief that anyone could have thrown away something that beautiful, bought the frame by promising to work off the debt. And that, of course, had been only the beginning. It had taken five years and more money than he wanted to think about to get the car running again. And now that it was his proudest possession, this woman was sneering at it.

"After Friday, you'll never have to ride in it again," he told her. "Get in."

"Yes, but I'll have to look at it. It's like living upstairs from Beelzebub."

"Thank you," he said, and when she got in the car, he slammed the door. Some women had no appreciation for the finer things in life, and Lord knew it was no surprise she was one of them.

"Where are we going?" she asked when they were on the road. He fished in his jacket pocket and handed her a note that said "Ring. Dress. Lunch."

"We need a ring," he told her, used to repeating everything to his classes even though they had a syllabus in front of them. "And a dress. And then we'll have lunch so we can talk about this." He looked over at all her yellow and blue fabric and winced. "We'll get a white dress."

Daisy scowled. "I like color."

Linc looked back to the road. "For this weekend, you're wearing white." He shot a glance at her for her reaction and caught her scowling harder. "And quit doing that. You could curdle milk with that face."

She sighed and smoothed out her frown. "I'm beginning to regret this."

For some reason, that made Linc clutch a little. "Think of the thousand dollars," he told her, remembering how grateful she'd been the night before.

She nodded. "And Annie."

The cat again. "Listen. I would have let you keep the cat anyway."

"Really?"

"Sure. You look like you could use a friend."

Daisy lifted her chin. "I have a friend. Several."

"Sorry. You just never seem to have much company." He looked over at her and saw her scowling again. "Cut that out."

Daisy obediently smoothed out her face. "Derek didn't like company. And after a while my company didn't like Derek, so they didn't come back."

"Derek." Linc remembered. "Thin blond guy. Played the stereo too loud."

Daisy nodded. "He's a musician. He's got hearing problems from standing too close to the speakers on-stage. That's how I met him. Somebody turned the amps up at a concert one night and he fell off the stage at my feet and cut his head, and I had a Band-Aid, and he said he'd never met anybody who'd brought a Band-Aid to a rock concert before."

Linc looked over at her, amazed. This had to be a story. "You're making this up."

Daisy scowled at him again. "I am not. He moved in a week later."

Linc moved his eyes back to the road, feeling exasperated. After one week she let some complete stranger move in. This woman had no common sense. Not that it was any of his business.

Come to think of it, though, what they were doing was pretty much Derek's business. Linc was never going to live with a woman, but if he ever did, he certainly wasn't going to let her pretend to be somebody else's fiancée. "Will Derek be upset about this thing you're doing for me?"

"He's gone."

Linc glanced at her, but she was obviously not going to explain. "Well, thanks for turning down the stereo. I really appreciate it."

"Derek took it with him when he went." Daisy looked out the car window, oblivious of his reaction.

It was none of his business, but he had to ask. "Was it his stereo?"

"No."

Linc shook his head. Derek must be a fool. A great apartment and a woman with Band-Aids who didn't care if he was deaf because he'd been too dumb to move away from a speaker. And then he'd stolen her stereo. How had he found it in that mess of an apartment? Her life was as big a mess as her apartment.

He pulled up in front of a small jewelry store. "Try not to lose your grip in there," he told her. "I'm a college professor, not a millionaire."

She nodded obediently and followed him into the dim coolness of the store.

Daisy bumped into Linc when he stopped in front of the case that held the diamonds. She peered around him. The stones sat there like ice on black velvet, and she shook her head and moved on. "Too cold. I like pearls."

"Thank you," Linc said, and she knew he thought she was saving him money. The truth was, she just liked pearls.

The pearls were much better, warm and glowing

and real. Linc pointed to one ring immediately, an old-fashioned carved band with a circle of small pearls surrounding a tiny sapphire center. "This one, the daisy," he told the clerk. Then he turned to Daisy and said, "It's a natural. Old-fashioned. Crawford will love it."

Daisy restrained herself from pointing out that he should give it to Crawford, then, since it wasn't her style at all. Her style was the one next to it, a heavy chased-silver band holding twisted free-form pearls. Still, he'd told her to develop some tact, and she was working on it. Lord knew he was paying enough for it. "Yes, that one is nice." She smiled at him. "But I like this one." She pointed to the silver band. "I like freshwater pearls."

"Forget it. The daisy ring," Linc told the sales-clerk.

The clerk frowned at Linc, and Daisy saw it. The light was dim in the store, and while he took her ring size, the clerk treated her as if she were an abused child. People had mistaken her age in dim light before, maybe she could get away with it here too. It was worth a try, if only to show this control freak she was nobody to mess with. She slipped her hand through Linc's arm. "All right, we'll take that ring now, honey." She beamed up at him innocently. "But when I'm eighteen, can I have the other one? Please, please?" She batted her eyelashes at him.

The clerk frowned even harder, and Linc looked dumbfounded.

Daisy transferred her beam to the clerk. "He's so good to me. I can't think why Mama and Daddy don't like him."

The clerk shook his head in disgust and went to ring the sale.

Daisy met Linc's eyes as innocently as she could.

He wasn't amused. "Listen, cupcake, you're cute, but there's no way you can pass for eighteen. Stop causing problems."

Daisy smiled at him sunnily. "You haven't seen anything yet. That guy thinks I'm underage. You pervert."

Linc scowled harder. "Part of the deal is that you cooperate."

"In Prescott," Daisy pointed out. "We're not in Prescott yet."

Back at the car, Linc held the door for her and checked his watch, frowning. Evidently they were off his timetable. Daisy gritted her teeth; she hated schedules because all they produced was efficiency and guilt, two of her least favorite things. And Linc didn't help things any when he got in the car and said, "Can we get a dress without you losing your grip on reality?"

Daisy met his eyes. "You never know."

"That's what I hate about this," Linc said, and put the car in gear.

Shopping for a dress took exactly fifteen minutes. Daisy pulled Linc into a thrift shop and took a white-on-white embroidered rayon dress off a sale rack at the back of the store. She walked toward him, watching as he surveyed the place, realized everything in it was used, and said "No," but she was ready for him. She'd been hanging out with him for only a very short time, but already she knew him like a book.

"Trust me," she said. "I tried this on once and put it back because it makes me look like a dweeb-brained virgin. It'll go great with the ring." She surveyed him with contempt. "It'll fulfill all your fantasies, Daddy."

The thrift store clerk looked at Linc with disgusted interest.

"Stop that," Linc told her, and bought the dress, as she knew he would, just to get them out of the store.

From there they went to a basement deli near the college for sandwiches. Daisy sat across from Linc and watched him eat, exasperated with him because of all he stood for, including white clothes and daisy rings. "So, tell me what I need to know to be your fiancée. What were you like as a kid? Where did you grow up?"

"A little place in Ohio. Sidney." Linc bit into his reuben sandwich with a great deal of enjoyment, and Daisy suddenly remembered Julia talking about how enthusiastic he was in bed. *Stop it,* she told herself. Remember the car. "Sidney who?"

Linc shook his head and swallowed. "No, that's the name of the town. We were the Sidney Yellow Jackets. I still have my football jacket if you want to wear it. Crawford would think that was great."

Daisy frowned. "Yellow Jackets? Like bees?"

He nodded. "Our colors were black and yellow."

Daisy stared at him, incredulous while he attacked his sandwich again. "The Killer Bees from Sidney, Ohio?"

He was unperturbed. "Hey, I got a football scholarship."

Daisy shook her head and picked up her own sandwich. It was turkey on sourdough and much healthier than Linc's reuben, which must have had at least four thousand fat grams, which for some reason did not make her turkey look any less boring next to it. "My husband, the Killer Bee," she said, thinking resentful thoughts about corned beef.

Linc went on, oblivious to her. "Ohio is a big football state."

"Does that make me the queen bee?"

"As a matter of fact, my scholarship was to Ohio State."

"Which would make you a drone."

"It wasn't a great scholarship."

"It would explain why you've got such boring taste."

"But it didn't really matter, because I had a full ride on an academic scholarship."

Daisy got a faraway look on her face. "We could live in a little cottage called The Hive."

Linc stopped. "Are you listening to me?"

Daisy batted her eyes at him. "Of course, my darling. You were a football hero and got a full ride to Ohio State. You dated the homecoming queen, you were president of your senior class, you were voted most likely to succeed, and your teachers adored you. And you lost your virginity as a sophomore after the first football game."

Linc blinked. "How did you know?"

Daisy looked smug. "You've got yuppie written all over you, sweetie. The only thing I'd never have guessed was that you were a Killer Bee." She bit into her sandwich, happy to have nailed him.

Linc put down his reuben and smiled at her. "You

were in Art Club. You were in Drama Club. You were in National Honor Society. You wore glasses and weird clothes. You wrote poetry; you got straight A's in English, and you dated guys who were very serious about Life. You didn't lose your virginity until college, and then it was a great disappointment. You've spent your entire life hoping that a former football star from Sidney, Ohio, would ask you to marry him and move to Prescott, Ohio, so you could have lots of kids and become a Republican."

Daisy swallowed and grinned at him. "You were doing pretty good until you got to the former football star from Sidney, Ohio."

"Well, for the weekend, pretend the rest is true too."

Daisy tried to understand him. He must have had a repressed childhood, the kind she would have had if she'd had to live with her father for more than summers. He probably had one of those pushy mothers. "Does your mother like me?"

"My mother doesn't like anybody, including me."

Daisy put her sandwich down, suddenly not hungry. "That's awful."

Linc shrugged. "She's not an emotional woman. She doesn't dislike me. I'm fine. She leaves me alone. I've seen guys whose mothers call every weekend to see if they're married yet."

"That's my mother." Daisy picked up her sandwich again.

"And your dad calls you 'cupcake.' " Linc took another bite of his reuben.

Fat chance. "My father doesn't call me anything," Daisy said. "What's your father like?"

Linc chewed and swallowed. "Dead."

The lousy memories of her father disappeared under an onslaught of sympathy, and she let her sandwich drop onto her plate. "Oh. Oh, Linc, I'm sorry."

He shook his head. "He died when I was thirteen. He got to see me make a touchdown in my first junior high game, though."

"Oh, good." Daisy thought of Linc alone at all his other games. The story built in her mind—the valiant young athlete looking at the empty place in the stands after every touchdown, searching for the father who wasn't there, who wasn't ever going to be there—and her eyes welled with tears.

"Stop it." Linc handed her a napkin. "That was twenty-five years ago. I barely remember what he looked like. Tell me about your father."

Daisy blotted her tears and pulled herself together. "There's not much to tell. He left."

You had to ask, didn't you? Linc told himself. "That must have hurt."

Daisy shrugged and swallowed. "He left when I was one. I'm over it now."

Linc tried to think of something sympathetic to say. "Oh."

"I used to spend my summers with him and he'd try to make me neat and well-behaved so I wouldn't embarrass him. When I turned sixteen, I wouldn't go anymore. So I haven't seen my father much since then."

"Oh." It sounded messy, and Linc really didn't want to talk about it. "So did your mom remarry?"

"No." Daisy fished a pickle from her sandwich with such elaborate unconcern that Linc knew she was upset. "She's waiting for my father to come back."

"What?"

"I know." Daisy nibbled her pickle. "Even when I was a little kid, I knew it wasn't going to happen. But she still thinks he'll come back. She just can't see reality."

So it's hereditary, Linc thought, but all he said was "She must have loved him very much."

Daisy looked thoughtful. "I don't know. It was very romantic the way they met. He saw her behind the counter in a flower shop she worked in, and he swept her off her feet and into his limo, and I guess they were really crazy about each other for a while, and then the crazy part wore off for him, and he got a good look at what he'd married and didn't like it." Daisy shrugged. "He's a very conservative person. Very proper, very serious." She met his eyes. "Like you." Linc wasn't sure what to say, but she went on. "And my mother's sort of . . . fluffy. I don't think she ever caught on that she wasn't what he wanted. I mean, from her point of view, she was doing all the right things, being a good little wife. He just wanted somebody more sophisticated, somebody who fit with his reality. So he found that somebody and left."

"Ouch."

"Yeah." Daisy sighed. "But she still thinks it's just this error he made, and sooner or later he'll remember she's his one true love." She shrugged.

"Sooner or later? How long has it been?"

"Thirty-three years."

"Your mother is nuts," Linc said, and winced. "Sorry. I didn't mean . . ."

"I don't think she's actually nuts," Daisy said. "I think she's just detached from reality. It's a coping skill." She met his eyes and read his mind. "I am not detached from reality. I'm perfectly capable of taking short vacations from it, but I always know how to get back."

"Good. Try not to go on vacation this weekend. What do I call your mother?"

"Pansy."

Linc looked appalled. "Why?"

"Because that's her name."

Linc shook his head in disbelief. "Okay. Your mother is Pansy. What's she like?"

Daisy thought about her mother. What could you say about Pansy? "She's little," Daisy said finally. "Nothing like me. Blond. Cute. Southern. She'd go bananas for this ring." Daisy narrowed her eyes at him. "She'd go bananas for you too. The big, dark, handsome Yankee come to steal her little magnolia away. Just like Rhett Butler."

Linc looked quelling. "Frankly, my dear, I never thought of you as a magnolia."

Daisy didn't quell. "I never thought of you as a Killer Bee either. The things you find out when you're engaged to someone. What's your mother's name?"

"Gertrude."

"Gertrude? For real? Gertrude Blaise?"

"Her maiden name was Gertrude Schmidt."

Daisy nodded. "A German. I knew it." She sucked in her breath suddenly. "Oh, my God, I can't possibly marry you."

Linc put his sandwich down, alarmed. "Why?"

"My name." Daisy invested the words with as much tragedy as possible.

"Daisy?"

"Daisy Blaise." She made a retching face. "Disgusting."

He grinned. "Cute. Sounds like a stripper."

"Maybe that's how we met." Daisy perked up. "I was stripping and—"

"*No.*"

"Okay, then." Daisy tried to make her voice reasonable. "How did we meet? We should meet cute."

"No, we shouldn't." Linc pointed a finger at her. "Forget the fiction. We met because we live in the same building. We lie as little as possible."

"That's no good. I'll think of something," Daisy said, and Linc said, "No, you will not," and went back to his sandwich.

"Okay." Daisy pushed her empty plate away, prepared to concentrate. "Brothers or sisters?"

"Two brothers, Wilson and Kennedy. Wil and Ken."

"Lincoln, Wilson, and Kennedy?"

"Dad believed in role models. What about you?"

"I believe in role models," Daisy said, getting ready to tell him about Rosa Parks, and then she realized that he meant her family. "Oh. Two stepsisters. Melissa and Victoria. Very chic."

"Got it." Linc finished his sandwich and looked at his watch.

Am I boring you? Daisy thought, but all she said was "Anything else you need to know?"

"What do you do for a living?"

Exactly what it says on my card on the mailbox, Daisy wanted to say, but she repressed it. Being around Linc meant repressing a lot. She didn't like it. "I paint and tell stories. Julia said you wrote a book once. What was it called?"

"The Nineteenth-Century Sporting Event as Social History."

"Catchy title. Who's going to play you in the movie?"

Linc looked at her with palpable calm. "Maybe I should just tell everyone in Prescott that you're mute."

Daisy grinned back. "I'll be good."

"Remember that. What do you paint?"

"Primitives."

"Primitives?"

Daisy thought about explaining it to him, telling him about the women she painted in the smallest, simplest shapes possible, surrounding them with the tiny details of their lives so that the simplicity became complexity, the way that the simplicity of their lives became complex when you looked at their hopes and fears and dreams and stories. Then she looked at Linc sitting across from her, logical and reasonable, and decided to forget it. This was obviously a man not interested in visual arts or in women's lives. "It's hard to explain, but I do them very well."

Linc nodded, clearly uninterested. "What else? How do you really earn a living?"

"I told you. Painting. Storytelling. I sell jewelry to an upscale craft store. I used to have some savings from when I was a teacher, but that's all gone now."

Linc looked nonplused. "How old are you?"

"I'll be thirty-five in September."

"You're thirty-five and you have no career and no steady income." Linc shook his head. "Who feeds you? The ravens?"

"I do all right." Reality was not the story Daisy wanted to talk about. "This is your fantasy," she told him. "I'm just along for the ride until midnight, when I turn into a pumpkin. Why don't you just tell me your story, and I'll memorize it, and we'll be done."

"Great," Linc said, and began to talk. It was so much worse than Daisy had imagined, full of plans for a woman in a designer apron and smiling, apple-cheeked children dressed in Baby Gap and a stuffy career in a stuffy town. The man had no imagination at all, and she was stuck in his story. Thank God it was only for twenty-four hours. If anyone had heard her, her storytelling career would have been over forever.

Linc finished the story, feeling much better about the whole situation. Daisy was obviously a bright woman, and his story sounded pretty good as he told it. For the first time, he thought the whole thing might actually work.

"That is without a doubt the worst story I've ever heard," Daisy said.

Linc bit back a reply. He needed her. He was going to have to put up with her for only one night. "Well, pretend you love it while we're in Prescott."

"No problem." Daisy tilted her head a little, dropped her chin, and opened her eyes wide. "I'm just thrilled to be here in Prescott, the cutest little town in Ohio and the perfect place to raise my two point four children, who'll all be going to Harvard on full academic scholarships. I can't tell you how excited I am."

She leaned forward a little and looked up at him under her lashes. He looked straight down the graceful line of her throat and into the gaping neckline of her ridiculous yellow dress and saw full, creamy curves. He jerked his startled eyes up to meet hers. She had a body. He'd missed that in all the clothes and the scowling, but she wasn't scowling now. She was smiling at him dreamily, the killer smile that had laid Guthrie low, her lips parted and soft. A wave of lust rolled over him. *She's nuts and she's messy and she irritates the hell out of you,* he told himself, but all he could see were those curves and that wide, lush smile.

"I can't wait," she repeated, and Linc said, "Stop that," and she laughed.

Linc stood up just to get away from her. "Come on, Magnolia. I have to get back to school."

When they were outside, Daisy rolled her eyes at the car again, but she behaved herself until they were halfway home, which gave him some time to recover. Then she put her hand on his arm and pointed. "Can we stop up there for a minute? Just a minute?"

He looked ahead to where she was pointing, at a craft boutique. It didn't seem like much to ask, and it would get her out of the car for a few minutes while he got his mind back where it belonged. "Sure." He checked the rearview mirror and pulled over. "Don't take too long. I have to teach in forty-five minutes."

Daisy nodded, took a deep breath, got out of the car, and walked into the store.

Linc watched her through the big plate-glass window and relaxed. When her mouth wasn't open and irritating him, and her dress wasn't gaping and inflaming him, Daisy Flattery was cute. He watched her

52   *Jennifer Crusie*

trek up to the counter, her ridiculous long skirt making her look like a kid playing dress-up. She asked for something, and the guy behind the counter leaned on the register, bored, and shook his head. Daisy said something else, and he shook his head again. Linc glanced at his watch and looked back at the guy. He was sneering. What was it with her? First Derek, now this guy. *This woman has an absolute affinity for jerks,* he thought, and got out of the car.

"Look, Howard." Daisy faced the store owner and tried to be tough. And mature. Mature was important. "You sold the last of my jewelry two weeks ago."

"I told you." Howard pressed his lips together with exaggerated patience. "Checks at the end of the month."

"But you didn't give me a check at the end of last month," Daisy pointed out. "And some of my pieces were sold by then."

"Checks at the end of the month." Howard looked up and beamed, and Daisy turned to see who had come in.

It was Linc, looking prosperous in his expensive suit. Linc, looking sort of big and dangerous, like a hit man. Only protective, which was nice. A big, dangerous, protective hit man.

Howard's voice oiled out from behind the register. "Can I help you, sir?"

The heck with mature. She'd never been any good at mature anyway. "You're in trouble, Howard," she told him, hooking her thumb over her shoulder at Linc. "This is my brother from New Jersey."

THREE

LINC AND HOWARD looked at her, stunned.

Daisy nodded solemnly at Howard. "He doesn't like me much, but he believes fair is fair, and he's against people who cheat innocent, hardworking women. I told him you wouldn't pay me even though you'd sold my stuff. I'm sorry, Howard, but a woman's got to do what a woman's got to do."

"Daisy." Linc's voice was cold with warning.

"Don't break his fingers, Linc," Daisy pleaded, not taking her eyes off Howard. "He's not a bad guy. He'll give me the money."

"Who are you trying to kid?" Howard sneered at her again.

"Wait a minute."

Daisy shot a glance at Linc. He'd turned his icy stare to Howard. *Oh, good.*

"There's no need to insult her," Linc told him. "If you owe her the money, pay her, but whatever you do, treat her like a lady."

Daisy felt warm all over. She'd never had a brother before. It was great.

Howard transferred his sneer to Linc. "Hey, she knows how this works."

"If you owe her the money—" Linc began again.

"I don't know who you really are, buddy," Howard interrupted, "but..."

Buddy? Daisy watched Linc's face darken. *Thank you, Howard, for being a consistent jerk,* she thought. An equal opportunity jerk. A jerk for all seasons.

"Give her the money, Howard," Linc said.

Daisy stole another glance at Linc. He looked mad. Big and mad. And it was all for her. Oh, good. Oh, really good.

"What?" Howard stepped back.

"I said, give her the money." Linc put both hands on the counter and loomed over him. "Pretend it's the end of the month and give her what you owe her."

Daisy looked at Howard, expecting him to sneer again, but he didn't. He was looking at Linc with healthy respect. And Linc wasn't looking much like a college professor, not with that jaw. He was looking like a thug with a very short fuse. She heard the register chime, and Howard shoved a handful of bills at her.

She counted it. "This is only seventy. You owe me a hundred and twenty, Howard."

"You're wasting our time, Howard," Linc said.

Howard shoved some more bills at Daisy.

Daisy counted some more. "This is too much." She put some of the bills back on the counter. "Now we're even."

"Great," Howard said, never taking his eyes off Linc.

"Well, I think so," Daisy said.

Out in the car, Daisy looked at Linc proudly. "My brother from Jersey."

Linc closed his eyes and wondered if there was insanity in his family. First "Yes, I have a fiancée" and now "Yes, I'm her brother from New Jersey." At least this time he hadn't actually said anything. This one wasn't his fault. He turned and glared at Daisy. "Don't ever do that again."

Daisy bounced a little on the seat as she looked at the bills fanned out in her hand. "That was terrific."

He pulled out into traffic and then looked at her, bouncing with happiness, and he was torn between killing her and jumping her, which only increased his annoyance. "Not *ever* again."

She beamed over at him. "You were great."

He glared at her harder. "I mean it. *Not ever again.*"

"All right." Daisy clutched her money and smiled at him, content. "Not ever again. My brother from Jersey is now dead."

He moved into the fast lane and picked up speed. What the hell did she think she was doing in there? What the hell did *he* think he was doing in there? Linc shook his head. The woman was a menace. Still, she didn't deserve the way that jerk had treated her. Whatever else Daisy Flattery did, he was sure she didn't ask for anything she didn't deserve. And Howard had been kicking her around just because he could. Linc hated bullies, having run across quite a few of them in his youth, people who thought because you were poor it was all right to push you around. It wasn't, and telling Howard that it wasn't had felt great. Making Howard's sneer disappear like dirty snow in the rain hadn't been the intelligent, mature, responsible thing to do, but it had been satisfying. And fun—

No, it hadn't. He stopped for a red light and glared at Daisy again. "Don't *ever* do that again."

She rolled her eyes, exasperated. "All *right*."

Linc made a sound between a groan and a snarl and stepped on the gas as the light turned green.

"You know," she said a few minutes later as he pulled into the driveway at their house, "I don't think you appreciate me."

"You're an acquired taste." He got out and held the car door open for her. "And unfortunately, we're not going to be together long enough for me to acquire that taste."

"That's not unfortunate." Daisy took his hand as he levered her out of the low-slung car seat. "Just because you acquired a taste for me doesn't mean I'd let you indulge it. You've just saved yourself a lot of frustration."

Linc looked down at her, fed up. "Trust me. If I acquired a taste, you'd let me indulge. I'm irresistible." He met her eyes, ready for battle, and she smiled at him, that bone-melting smile. Combined with the surge of adrenaline he'd gotten from rescuing her from Howard and the surge of lust he got every time he looked down her dress, her smile wiped all thought temporarily from his mind and breathing was suddenly difficult.

"Don't do that," Linc said.

"Don't underestimate me," Daisy said.

"That would be a mistake," Linc agreed, and got in the car without looking at her again.

On the plane the next day, Linc was relieved to see that Daisy was a different woman. She sat quietly in her white dress with her ankles crossed and her chin down, and she didn't say a word. During the takeoff, she'd held his hand, and he'd though that it was a nice touch until he noticed her hands were like ice and her knuckles were white. She was cutting off the circulation to his fingers.

"Are you scared?"

Her voice was only one notch above a whisper. "I hate flying."

"Why didn't you say so?"

"One thousand dollars."

"Flying is statistically safer than driving, so you can relax." Linc pried her fingers loose. "Concentrate on the money. Your rent is paid, by the way. I sent it directly to Guthrie so he wouldn't evict you while we were gone."

Daisy clenched her hands in her lap. "I know you paid it. He called."

Linc winced. "I should have thought of that. I

suppose he thinks I'm keeping you. Did he threaten to evict you for immoral behavior?"

Daisy shook her head a little. "No. I'm not sure, but I think he offered to take over for you if things didn't work out between us."

"What?"

"I think he propositioned me. I'm not sure. He hems and haws a lot."

"The creep." Linc took her hand again and thought about what louses men could be to defenseless women like Daisy. "Would you like me to break his fingers?"

Daisy rolled her eyes at him. "Linc, he knows you're not my brother from New Jersey."

"I'll break his fingers anyway, the old goat." Linc was outraged. Poor Daisy. She was such a nice kid.

He stopped. The story was working. Daisy wasn't a nice kid; she was a hippie from hell. But she had even him thinking she was a sweet little thing. He looked down at her. She did look sort of gormless, sitting there with one hand curled in her lap, the other crushing his again whenever they hit an air pocket.

"Did he upset you?"

"Guthrie?" Daisy shook her head and loosened her grip. "Oh, no. I just don't like flying." After a couple of minutes during which no air pockets attacked the plane, she peered up at him. "How about you? Are you nervous about the speech?"

"No." Linc thought about the speech and the party afterward and shifted in his seat.

"Well, then, what are you nervous about?"

"What?"

He looked down at her, annoyed, but she met his eyes calmly, and he realized he wasn't breathing again. He drew in a deep breath through his nostrils, and Daisy said, "I hate it when you do that. If you don't want to talk to me, don't, but don't flare your nostrils at me like William F. Buckley—"

"What? I'm not flaring my nostrils—"

"—because that's just rude."

"—I'm breathing."

Daisy didn't look convinced, so he went on. "When I get tense, I hold my breath. It's a bad habit, so I concentrate on breathing deliberately through my nose to make sure I don't pass out."

Daisy blinked at him. "You're kidding. You forget to breathe?"

Linc turned away to look out the window. "It's a very common reaction to stress."

"I didn't think you even had stress," Daisy said. "It doesn't seem in character."

"It isn't," Linc said shortly. "That's why I breathe. Can we talk about something else?"

"Sure." Daisy cocked her head at him. "If you're not worried about the speech, why are you stressed?"

"Look," Linc began, planning to tell her to mind her own business, but then he realized she was right. He was wound so tight, he was going to be breathing through his hair at any minute. "I think it's the lying," he said finally. "I'm not a liar. I've never lied before. And now I not only lied, I dragged you into this whole mess and you're lying too. It's not right."

"It's not a lie," Daisy said. "It's a story."

Linc looked at her, exasperated. "That's semantics. They're the same thing."

"No, they're not." Daisy scowled at him, and Linc remembered too late that she told stories for a living; he'd just called her a professional liar.

"I didn't mean to insult you—"

"Lies are untrue," Daisy said with all the sureness of Moses laying down the law. "Stories are unreal, but they're true. They're always true."

Linc shook his head. "I still don't see the difference. I'm sorry, but—"

"Listen." Daisy leaned forward and gripped his arm to hold his attention. "If you tell a lie, you're deliberately telling an untruth. If you'd told them you'd published six books, or that you'd taught at Yale, or that you'd won the Pulitzer, that would have been a lie. You'd never tell a lie. You're too honest."

"Daisy, I told them I was engaged to you. That was a lie."

"No." Daisy shook her head emphatically. "You didn't tell them anything about me. You told them you wanted to get married and settle down in Prescott and raise kids."

"Well, that's a lie," Linc said, but he could see where she was going. "I told them what they wanted to hear."

"Yes, but it was what you wanted to hear too." Daisy settled back in her seat. "Sometimes stories are just previews of coming truths. I bet you really do want that deep down inside your repressed academic soul. I bet your subconscious just wormed its way to the truth and laid it all out when you were too stressed and preoccupied with breathing to keep an eye on it."

"Very cute," Linc said. "Would you like to explain the Alizarin Crimson, the daisy ring fiasco, and my brother from Jersey now?"

Daisy shrugged. "Sure. Annie is an original cat, definitely one of a kind, and she's reddish, so telling Guthrie she was an Alizarin Crimson was true in its own way. And you were treating me like a child bride in the store, not letting me pick out my own ring, so I became one. That one was really your story, not mine. And the brother part..." She looked up again, a little shy. "I think I just wanted somebody to rescue me, you know? Howard was being such a louse, and I just wanted somebody to stick up for me, the way a brother would. I get really tired of fighting my own battles. And then you came in, and I knew you'd stick up for me. I just knew you would. And you knew it too. That's how I know it's true, even if it isn't real. You walked right into my story."

Linc pulled back. "I did not know it."

"Yes, you did." Daisy leaned her head back on the seat. "You could have denied everything, or told me to shut up, or dragged me from the store, or walked out. Really, you could have done almost anything." She turned her head to meet his eyes. "Instead, you were my brother from New Jersey. You knew it was true too."

"I'm still not buying this," Linc told her, but he was irrationally cheered. Maybe he hadn't lied. Maybe it had been a glimpse of the future. Maybe—

The plane hit another air pocket, and Daisy clutched his hand. "How much longer to Prescott?"

"About fifteen minutes to the Dayton airport. About another forty-five to Prescott by car."

"Are we renting a car?"

"No, Crawford said he'd come pick us up."

"The dean? You must really rate."

"Not me. I told him all about you. He can't wait. He calls you 'Little Daisy.' "

Daisy closed her eyes. "Oh, no."

"So this is Little Daisy!" Crawford beamed at her. "Even sweeter than I'd pictured her!"

He looked like an anti-Santa Claus, leering instead of beaming, and Daisy disliked him on sight. So this was what she had to impress so Linc could get the job. Just her luck. She ducked her head and smiled, and Crawford almost fell over backward from the wattage.

"Lincoln, you are one lucky dog." Crawford put his arm around Daisy, who stifled a shudder.

Linc smirked. "Thank you, sir."

Crawford's hand slid down over her hip.

Daisy wanted to kill them both. *This is what happens when you let other people tell the story,* she told herself. *Don't do that again.*

Crawford had them out to the parking lot in no time. He waved them toward a big maroon Cadillac, and a chubby blonde waved back frantically. "This is my little woman," he said as she disentangled herself from the front seat and got out of the car. "Chickie, honey, this is Linc and Daisy."

Chickie leaped on Linc. "Daddy didn't tell me how handsome you were," she said, and hugged him, and Daisy thought, *Good, let him get groped for a change*. Then Chickie turned on Daisy and her bright, vague smile widened. "And you must be Daisy! I declare, you're a picture!" She threw her arms around Daisy, engulfing her in a cloud of Chanel No. 5 and gin. It smelled a lot like a drink Daisy had thrown up once at a college mixer.

Daisy fought her way free. "Well, I'm just so delighted to meet you, Chickie. We'll have to sit down later and have a girls' talk."

Linc closed his eyes. *Pouring it on too thick,* Daisy thought.

"We will, we will." Chickie beamed and hugged her again.

"Well, let's go." Crawford wasn't having any fun and his leer was getting tired. "Let's go."

Linc held the front passenger door open for Chickie and she was visibly thrilled. Then he held the back door for Daisy, and she resisted the urge to kick him on the ankle. "You're such a darling," she said instead, and batted her eyes at him. "I just love you."

"Don't push it," Linc said under his breath.

"Isn't she just the sweetest?" Chickie said to Crawford when they were all in the car.

"Yes, she is." Crawford leered over the seat at Daisy. "You're a lucky dog, Lincoln."

By now Linc's smirk was gone and his smile was pasted on. "Yes, sir."

This is going to be the car ride from hell, Daisy thought, and she was right. By the time Crawford had driven them to Prescott, helped them drop their things off at the motel, and then driven them out to the college, they'd heard what a lucky dog Linc was a dozen times, and Linc had said, "Yes, sir," another dozen, and Chickie had never stopped babbling. Daisy was ready to scream, but she told herself that if she could keep smiling long enough to get into the lecture room, the Crawfords would have to shut up so Linc could give his speech. It was the only time in her life that she'd ever looked forward to a speech.

As it turned out, she wasn't destined to hear it.

"You two go on along," Chickie said when they were standing beside the car. "I'm going to show Daisy all of Prescott." She flapped her hand at them. "Go on. Just go on."

Crawford frowned. "The faculty should meet Daisy. Professor Booker should meet Daisy. I—"

"They can meet her at the party tonight." Chickie fished her car keys out of her purse and waved Daisy toward the front seat. "You go on."

"Daisy would like to hear her future husband's

speech," Crawford said, and the annoyance in his voice was plain.

Chickie faltered. "Would you?" she asked, turning to Daisy.

Daisy's choices were Crawford and a speech on history, or Chickie and a look at a small town. It was a toss-up until she saw the uncertainty in Chickie's eyes; whatever else Chickie was, she was vulnerable. "Oh, I've heard that speech a thousand times," she told Crawford sweetly. "Linc rehearses everything with me."

Chickie's hand dropped to her side as she shook her head in admiring wonder. "Isn't that just darling? Aren't the two of you just darling?"

"I think so." Daisy stretched up and kissed Linc on the cheek. "Knock them dead, darling."

"Thank you." Linc bent to kiss her cheek in return and whispered in her ear, "Behave, brat."

She smiled at him and waved, Chickie-style, and got in the front seat, rewarded not only by his look of trepidation but also by Crawford's scowl. Good, two with one blow. It was starting to be her story after all. She turned and smiled as Chickie slid into the driver's seat. "This was a very good idea," she told her. "You're so thoughtful."

Chickie patted her knee and then put the key in the

ignition. "Not at all, I'm just selfish. I just wanted to get to know you all by myself."

As Chickie pulled the car out into the street, it lurched a little. Third gear not first, Daisy guessed, and turned her attention to Prescott.

The university had made the little town an odd mixture of cosmopolitan and provincial, with interesting combinations like a gourmet grocery next to an old-fashioned hardware store and a diner straight from the fifties. The one theater had a sagging marquee and an improbably chartreuse and hot pink facade, but it was showing the latest Tarentino, and the coming attractions posters promised a Bergman revival, and an old Walter Matthau and Elaine May movie called *A New Leaf*.

"I love that movie!" Daisy told Chickie. "Have you ever seen it? He marries her for money even though she's hopelessly disorganized and then he falls for her anyway. It's wonderful."

"I wish you were going to be here for it," Chickie said with real regret. "We could go together, just like a mother and daughter. Wouldn't that be fun?"

"Yes," Daisy said, a little taken aback to find herself in a story Chickie had obviously started without her.

"But you probably won't get here before fall since Linc still has to teach at his old job." Chickie sighed, and then brightened. "But there'll be other movies we can go to when you get here. Lots of them."

"If Linc gets the job," Daisy reminded her, but Chickie just patted her knee again. The car swerved in response, and Chickie transferred her attention back to the road, and that's when Daisy saw the art gallery.

"Tell me about that," she said, pointing to the wood facade that said GALLERY in gold lettering, and Chickie slowed down and said, "Oh, that's Bill's gallery. He started it over thirty years ago and it's very successful now. He has shows four times a year and all these big art people from New York come out to see his latest discoveries."

All the breath left Daisy's body in one long whoosh. "Discoveries?"

Chickie nodded. "He likes showcasing new artists, so two of his shows, the ones in January and July, are always about new people. He's been written up in all the big art magazines. He showed me the articles. They even had color pictures."

This is not your story, Daisy warned herself, but it was too late. It had been too late since she'd seen the gallery. The universe was doing everything but dropping a big sign in front of her that said *This is it, this is your next move.* Only it wasn't. *This is really cruel,* she thought, but she couldn't think of anyone outside of fate and the cosmos to blame.

Chickie picked up speed once they were past the gallery. "We can go sometime if you like art. I don't understand most of it, but I like Bill, and he doesn't make me feel dumb if I don't understand it."

"Well, of course not," Daisy said, momentarily jerked out of her dream. "Why would he?"

"Some people do," Chickie said vaguely, and Daisy thought of overbearing Crawford and wondered what living with that kind of disapproving, domineering man would do to a woman. Probably drive her to drink.

She put her hand over Chickie's. "Then they're lousy people and you shouldn't pay attention to them."

"Oh." Chickie blushed with pleasure. "Well, I don't know much, you know. I never went to college. I'm just a wife."

Daisy scowled. "We need to talk, Chickie. You are not just a wife."

Chickie patted Daisy's hand. "Well, that's just sweet of you, sugar, but that's pretty much what I am." She waved her hand at the window and said, "Now, this is a nice neighborhood to start out in," and Daisy realized they'd left the downtown and turned into a side street of old houses in various stages of repair. One had a sign in front that said PRESCOTT VETERINARY.

"The houses here are reasonable, and it's walking distance of the campus," Chickie told her.

And the vet's, Daisy thought. Nice and close for Liz and Annie. Except she wasn't going to be living here.

Then they turned down Tacoma Street, and she saw the house. It was a slightly tumbledown Victorian cottage with diamond panes in the front window and a big front porch with most of the gingerbread missing, and a picket fence that needed paint badly, and—best of all—a For Sale sign in front of it. "*Oh,*" she said, and Chickie stopped the car.

"That one?" Chickie looked doubtful. "Honey, it's in awful shape."

"I could fix it," Daisy said. "If the foundation's good, and it's not loaded with termites, I can fix everything else. I'm an artist. I can fix anything."

Chickie perked up. "You're an artist? Well, isn't that interesting? Linc didn't tell us that. Wait until I tell Bill."

"I'd paint it yellow," Daisy went on, half to distract Chickie and half because she was starting to love this story. "With blue and white trim. And I'd put the gingerbread back up. See where there's still some left at the side? I could use that as a pattern and cut more. It would be so beautiful."

Chickie looked back at the house, squinting to see it through Daisy's eyes. "Wouldn't you like something new?"

"*No,*" Daisy said with passion. "People throw away too many things because they always want new. But if you look at old things, they have history and personality and spirit. The things that I have that I love best are the old things that I've rescued. They have stories of their own, and then I fix them up and they're part of my story too." She looked back at the house, seeing the proportions under the peeling grayish paint, and the light that would certainly flood through the long, dingy windows once she'd cleaned them. Liz would stretch out and sleep on the hardwood floors Daisy knew were inside, and Annie could climb the porch rail and screech at people and birds. And Julia could come to visit.... "I could make that house a wonderful part of my story."

"I'd like to see that," Chickie said softly, still looking at the house. She sounded wistful, and then she turned to look at Daisy. "I'd like to watch you fix that house. Would that be all right?"

Daisy swallowed at the loneliness in Chickie's voice. "Sure," she said, hating herself for lying. "Of course, we don't know if Linc will get the job—"

Chickie turned back to the house. "He'll get the job." Her voice sounded grim with determination, and Daisy had a feeling that even if Linc had just given the most abysmal speech of his life, Chickie would see to it that Crawford hired him. If only the whole thing hadn't been a lie—no, a *story*—she'd have felt better.

If it had been true, she'd have felt wonderful, coming to live in this little town, in this little house, with a vet a block away and a great movie theater nearby and a gallery that might show her work in a couple of years, and a husband like Linc to take care of her—

That last thought brought her back to earth. A husband like Linc would take care of her, but he'd also make her be something she wasn't and then he'd probably make her feel guilty if she slipped. He'd be her father all over again. It was a story, but it was also a fairy tale.

"Yellow," Chickie said, still staring at the house. "I can just picture it. With lilacs out in front."

"Lilacs would be beautiful," Daisy said, seeing the purple contrasting with the yellow house and blending with the blue trim, and for a moment they both shared the picture and the story. "Lilacs would be perfect."

"Will be perfect," Chickie corrected her, and Daisy closed her eyes in regret.

Linc's presentation went the way all his presentations did: smoothly, clearly, and professionally. He could see approval in the eyes of his audience, particularly in the eyes of a trim little blonde in the front row. *Definitely my type,* he thought, and then he stopped. Not now she wasn't. Now he was engaged to Daisy. But in the fall, if he got the job, when he wasn't engaged...

Make a note to get to know the blonde in the fall, he told himself, trying not to feel guilty since there was no reason to, but somehow feeling guilty anyway.

The question and answer period after the talk was vigorous but supportive; most people weren't arguing with him as much as asking for more information, particularly the blonde, who seemed very intelligent and very interested in more than his speech. Even Booker thawed and told him he'd done good work. For a moment, surrounded by approving people, he wished that Daisy were there to see him do well, so that she'd know that he really was good. He would have liked to look up and see her smiling at him, just as if the story were true, just for that moment.

Then Crawford shook his hand and said, "That's a

fine little woman you have there. Chickie thinks she's just super."

Linc felt exasperated with him. The man had a university to run, for God's sake, and he was obsessing over faculty wives. "Well, I think she's super too."

"You know, she's just going to love living here in Prescott." Crawford winked, and Linc stiffened in surprise before he smiled back at Crawford with new appreciation.

My God, he thought. *She did it. I'm in.*

FOUR

CRAWFORD DROPPED LINC at the motel, and Linc shook his hand again in genuine gratitude. "I appreciate this, sir. More than you can know."

"Well, we appreciate you too, son," Crawford said. "And we surely do appreciate Daisy."

"Oh, we all do that," Linc said, his exasperation considerably lessened by his success. When Crawford finally drove away, he went to find her and give her the good news.

He opened the door to the motel room and saw her standing by the bed in her slip. She turned, lifting her chin in silent question about the speech, and he opened his mouth to tell her and then stopped, hit by the impact of Daisy undressed. Daisy would never make a model—too much bust, too much hip, too much everything—but she could make him lose his train of thought in an instant, even in a slip as opaque and virginal as the one she was wearing.

"How'd the speech go?" she asked, apparently unaware she was blowing his mind, and he came back to the present and said, "We did it. I got it."

"I knew it!" Daisy threw herself at him, and he caught her, surprised that she cared so much, and then distracted by how much warm softness she was pressing against him. "You are going to *love* it here," she told him, and he looked down at her in his arms and lost his train of thought again.

She was so round against him that he closed his eyes for a minute, trying to keep his sanity, and when he opened them she was looking up at him.

"You okay?"

His eyes slid past her face to her slip, made of white cotton with little pink flowers embroidered on it, and to the curve of her breasts pressed against him. She was warm and happy for him, and he didn't know what to do about it, so he held his breath while he coped.

She said, "Breathe, Blaise," and he took a deep breath and stepped back. "I'm fine."

Daisy sat down on the edge of one of the double

beds, still glowing, and her slip rode up her thighs. She had excellent long legs that she stretched out in front of her as she talked. "Chickie kept hinting all afternoon, but I couldn't believe it. Are you going to tell me what happened? Your speech must have been great."

"It wasn't just the speech." Linc sat down on the end of the other bed, trying to keep his eyes somewhere in the vicinity of her forehead. "Crawford didn't give a damn about the speech, although Booker did." The memory of the speech came back and he forgot Daisy had a body while he reveled in his victory again. "Booker loved the speech, but Crawford was hooked the moment you smiled at him. Thank God this college has such a small hiring committee. Make sure you tell him you love Prescott tonight at the party."

"I do." Daisy moved back into the center of the bed and stretched her legs out, crossing her ankles. "You should have seen the tour Chickie gave me."

Linc looked at her legs again. Somebody should do her a favor and burn all those long skirts. She had terrific legs. And they went all the way up.

Think of something else, he told himself, and looked at her face. "Crawford is crazy about you."

"I think he's just plain crazy, period." Daisy rolled off the bed and Linc tried not to look at her round butt as she slid to her feet. She headed to the bathroom, picking up her dress as she went. "I feel sorry for his poor wife."

"Chickie?" Linc was confused. "Why?"

"She's so lonely." Daisy's voice floated back to him. "She's just dying to have a surrogate daughter, and if their marriage was any good, she wouldn't need one. She'd have him to talk to." She came back out, zipping up the virgin dress as she walked, and he felt confused again, remembering the slip and the body under it at the same time he registered that she looked like a child. "I can't get over how you look in that dress. I feel like a child molester."

Daisy hesitated. "Do I look bad?"

"No." He tried to analyze how she did look. "Just provocative. Like a hot fairy tale. Sort of like Cinderella in heat."

He had a momentary vision of bouncing Daisy on the bed, sliding his hand up her hip, feeling her underneath him as those long legs—

"Linc?"

Make a note to stay out of motel rooms with Daisy, he told himself. "Nothing," he told her, and went to get ready for the party.

• • •

Daisy saw the Crawford house as Tara North: big columns, lots of drapery, flowers, gardens, statuary, everything that spelled opulent living, all in pink and white. "I do declare," she said to Linc under her breath, and he whispered back, "Behave, Magnolia."

She really tried.

Crawford practically drooled down her neckline, and said, "You really are a daisy," and she smiled back, even when he patted her rear end. *A thousand dollars is not enough,* she thought, but a deal was a deal. Professor Booker seemed a little staggered at first and then welcomed her politely. "You're not at all what I expected," he told her, and she smiled at him, turning on the charm as ordered. He blinked once, and then introduced her to his wife, Lacey, who was open and warm in her welcome and got a real smile in exchange. Later Booker moved to one side of the room and laughed quietly into his drink until Lacey nudged him with her elbow, and Daisy thought, *We're not fooling either one of them,* and liked them even more. A professor with a long, mournful face introduced himself. "I'm Evan York. History. Interesting dress. It probably won't wash well." His smile was brief but genuine, and Daisy liked him a lot too. There was something endearing about anyone that depressed.

There was nothing endearing about the last professor who introduced herself, a small blonde with a lovely face. "I'm Caroline Honeycutt, from the history department. I love your dress. Really." She smiled up at Daisy and managed to make it seem like she was smiling down. "And you must be so proud of Lincoln. His paper was brilliant. What do you think of his theory of the impact of the ring on social barriers?"

"I'm all for it," Daisy said, and Caroline's smile widened.

"Ah, you're not a historian," Caroline said. "Forgive me."

"You bet," Daisy said, but she thought, *I don't like you.* She liked Caroline even less when she slithered over to Linc and began to smile up at him. Really up at him, because she was little. And blond. Like Julia. And probably like all of Linc's other women. Not that it mattered. Linc smiled back, tall, dark, and gorgeous, looking down at tiny little Caroline.

Daisy gritted her teeth. There was no reason to be jealous. This was all just a story, and it wasn't even her story. No matter how much she loved Prescott and liked the people she met and wanted to save Chickie, it wasn't true. She and Linc were only pretending to be engaged.

But he wasn't pretending very well, the jerk.

Daisy decided to do the adult thing and ignore them while she concentrated on what Linc was paying her a thousand dollars to do. So she talked with Crawford, keeping out of range of his hands. She talked with Evan, radiating cheer to counteract his gloom. She talked with Lacey, sharing stories about Liz and Annie when she found out that Lacey loved animals too. She talked with Crawford again, because when she turned around he was there. She talked with Booker, sharing his admiration for Linc. She talked with someone from the English department who'd come for the drinks, sharing his annoyance that the mushroom canapes were gone. She talked with Crawford, because when she turned around he was there again. Crawford was growing from an annoyance to a real problem. She looked around for Linc to rescue her, but he was gone, and Daisy felt her temper rise.

If he's with that skinny midget Caroline, she thought, *I'm going to take steps.*

Linc was seriously confused.

On the one hand, he had Prescott for sure; Crawford had taken him aside when they arrived at the party and together with Booker had made him the formal offer which Linc had accepted so promptly that they had all beamed.

Then things began to get weird. It couldn't be the story, he told himself. After all, it was his story. No, it was more like slipping reality. There was Caroline Honeycutt, for example, logical, intelligent, and more than interested in him, exactly his kind of woman. And then there was Daisy, intuitive and unpredictable, scowling at him and charming everybody else, exactly not his kind of woman. So it was disconcerting that his eyes kept going back to Daisy instead of staying on Caroline. *It was seeing her in that slip,* he told himself. He'd stick close to Caroline, and he'd remember that he liked thin, lithe women dressed in designer suits and black lingerie, not round, tall women dressed in secondhand clothes and white slips with pink flowers, for God's sake, and then he wouldn't fall into the story and think about taking Daisy back to the motel and consummating his new job with his wife-to-be-who-wasn't.

Make a note not to tell any more stories, he told himself, and when Caroline joined him, he threw all his attention onto her and reality.

By midnight Daisy felt that if she flashed her smile one more time, her eyeballs would roll out and her cheeks would split. And it didn't help that every time she turned around, Linc was with Caroline.

"Linc." She walked up beside him, smiling.

He was talking with Caroline again and he ignored her.

"Linc?" She tugged on his sleeve, still smiling.

Caroline looked up at her and smiled patronizingly. "You are just too darling for words."

Daisy narrowed her eyes. "Don't be bitchy, dear, it ages you."

Linc took her arm and steered her away from a startled Caroline.

"What are you doing?" he whispered.

Daisy put her hands on her hips and glared up at him. "I'm going back to the motel. This is my idea of hell, but I have been good for five excruciating hours, and now it's time for me to be set free. Take me home, cupcake, or I'll turn into a pumpkin right here before their very eyes. And the first one I show my real self to will be that patronizing anorexic dwarf with the bad bleach job."

"Hold on." Linc patted her shoulder a little frantically. "I will get you out, I swear, but it will take some time. We'll have to say good-bye. Can you stand it another fifteen minutes?"

"Just about."

It took them half an hour before they'd said all

their good-byes and the Crawfords would let them go. Daisy figured that unless Linc did something incredibly stupid, he was in. Then she saw him with Caroline again, holding her hand, looking into her eyes, saying good-bye. Laying the groundwork for laying Caroline next year. Well, the hell with them both. They deserved each other.

And then she turned and saw the expression on Chickie's face as Chickie watched them.

Chickie must have watched her husband with a lot of women, Daisy thought. *And Chickie hasn't attached to Linc, she's attached to me. The daughter she never had.*

Linc, you dummy.

Daisy moved up beside Chickie and sighed. "It's so sad."

Chickie put her arm around Daisy and glared in Linc's direction. "Men!"

Daisy looked surprised. "Oh, no. He's not interested in Caroline that way. It's just that she looks like his little sister. His little sister . . . Gertrude."

Chickie stopped, taken aback. "Oh?"

"You see . . ." Daisy leaned closer as her mind raced ahead. "He adored her, and she died very young."

"Oh, no." Chickie was horrified.

Daisy got a faraway look in her eye. "They loved

each other very much. He called her his little cupcake. She called him"—Daisy's imagination faltered. What the hell had she called him—"Honest Abe. After the president. Lincoln, you know?"

She saw Chickie frown and decided to retrench a little. "As a joke. She called him that as a joke. They joked around a lot."

Chickie nodded.

Daisy tried to recapture the thread of her story. "And then one day—" She paused. How was she going to kill off this nauseating little creep? Disease? Murder? Act of God? How would she like Caroline to go? "She was hit by a truck."

"Oh, my heavens." Chickie's hand went to her mouth.

It was a good thing Chickie was so full of gin. This was not one of Daisy's best efforts. "And so, Linc is just naturally drawn to be kind to small blondes because they remind him of his little cupcake. Little Gertrude."

"Oh." Chickie clutched at her, touched.

Linc finally let go of Little Gertrude's hand and turned to find them watching him. Chickie sniffled. Daisy wiggled her fingers at him.

He walked over to them and took Daisy's hand. "Well, it's midnight, so I've got to get Cinderella home."

Chickie clutched his arm. "You poor, poor boy."

Linc looked at the gin glass in Chickie's other hand and nodded. "Absolutely. We'll see you tomorrow."

He put his arm around Daisy and pulled her out the door.

"What was that all about?" he asked Daisy as they went out to the car.

Daisy beamed at him. "I'll tell you later, but it's nothing to worry about." Linc looked at her warily, and she added, "Unless you were hoping to sleep with Caroline someday. That would be bad."

"Daisy—" Linc said, but then Crawford joined them and cut him off.

Daisy got into the car and smiled all the way back to the motel.

Half an hour later Daisy came out of the motel bathroom wearing an oversize white T-shirt and saw Linc sitting on the opposite bed with his shirt off. *Merciful heavens,* she thought, and then she stopped thinking in words and went to pictures. Moving pictures.

He scowled at her across her bed. "Why can't I sleep with Caroline someday?"

So much for fantasy; he was still obsessing on the overbred blonde. "Because she reminds you of your poor dear sister Gertrude." Daisy pulled back the covers and climbed into her bed. "Chickie would consider it incest."

Linc tensed, wariness in every beautiful muscle. "I don't have a sister named Gertrude."

Daisy nodded, enjoying his torment. If she had to look at his body and suffer, then he should have to look into her mind and do the same. It was only fair. "I know. She died young. Tragically. She—"

"Daisy!"

Daisy stuck her chin out. "That's why you hold hands with blond midgets instead of paying attention to your fiancée. I had to explain to Chickie because she thought you were cheating on me in front of me. The way Crawford probably does with her. Understand?"

Linc froze. "Oh."

"You used to call her your little cupcake. She called you Honest Abe."

Linc looked confused. "Chickie?"

"No, dear Little Gertrude."

Linc started to laugh, and Daisy had to grin with him. "And Chickie bought this?" he asked her.

Daisy's grin faded as she remembered. "She was drunk. She drinks way too much, but it's because she's so unhappy. She'd stop if she had somebody to talk to."

Linc's grin disappeared too. "Did she tell you that? How much did you talk? What did you tell her? What did you do this afternoon?"

Daisy stuck her chin out. "We just looked at Prescott. But I can tell. She's a good person, she's just so, so lonely."

Linc leaned forward. "Don't get caught up in this story. It's not true, remember?"

"I know," Daisy said.

He stood up to get ready for bed, and she closed her eyes because he was so near. "I appreciate everything you did today, don't think I don't," he told her. "I know that you were the deciding factor. You got me this job, and I appreciate it."

How much? she thought, and considered asking him to show it, but only for a second. Then sanity returned, and she said, "My pleasure," and rolled away from him before she did anything dumb.

Once they were on the plane the next day, they both relaxed. "You did it." Daisy leaned her head back and sighed. "I can't believe it. You did it. I'm so proud," she said, and he felt warm because he had done well, which had happened before, and because somebody was proud of him for it, which hadn't happened in a long time. She looked at him with pride and affection and friendship, and he was a little sorry that it was all over. They'd reached The End, and they'd both live happily ever after apart, the only way people as different as they were could live happily ever after. Daisy would go back to dressing like a leaky Magic Marker, and he would go to Prescott.

Prescott.

He was really going. Because of Daisy.

"Let me give you something to thank you." He took her hand and squeezed it. "You can have anything you want."

Daisy hesitated long enough that he bent to see her face better, and then she turned to him. She pulled her hand from his grasp and tugged the daisy ring off her finger and handed it to him, smiling up at him at the same time, which took some of the sting off the move, although not enough. His hand closed around the ring automatically.

"Just promise me that I'll never have to see Crawford again," Daisy said.

"You've got it," Linc said as the sapphire in the ring cut into his palm. "That I can promise."

FIVE

Linc spent the rest of the spring finishing up loose ends at the university and getting ready to move. He saw Daisy in the apartment foyer and thought about asking her out for pizza or something else mundane that wouldn't signal "date," but it seemed better to just keep nodding and moving past her so that he wouldn't get caught up in the story again. Daisy was a hard habit to kick, he'd discovered, even after only three days. She was sloppy and round and uncontrolled, and she brought warmth and chaos into his life, and he was having a hard time forgetting her. Especially in the middle of the night when he'd remember the motel room. Sometimes the only thing that got him through those middle-of-the-nights was the memory of how awful she could be. She'd brought him more anxiety in the three days he'd spent with her than all the other women he'd ever known put together. But she'd also brought him Prescott. He sent her flowers to thank her before he left. Then he packed and moved to Ohio.

He bought a small Victorian house Chickie found for him on Tacoma Street about a mile from campus. Linc preferred a more modern look to his housing, but this place had been rented to students for forty years and needed a lot of repair, so it was a bargain, or at least as much of a bargain as any house could be in a college town. The structure was solid and the rooms were airy and the holes in the walls could be fixed with spackle and paint. "I can't thank you enough," he told Chickie when she'd shown him through it. "You found me a great deal."

Chickie beamed and patted the oak mantel. "Isn't it darling? And Daisy will have such fun fixing it up." She leaned forward. "I know you men. You wouldn't care where you lived, but Daisy needs something sweet and pretty."

"Right," Linc said and thought *wrong*. Daisy needed therapy and a full-time keeper, but that wasn't his problem.

Chickie turned to gaze around at the oak wood-work again, obviously picturing Daisy dusting or doing other housewifely things, and Linc winced at how happy she looked. She still thought she was getting a surrogate daughter. He felt ashamed for leading her on. But Daisy would probably have been a great disappointment to Chickie, since he was fairly sure she never dusted. And he'd tell her eventually that Daisy wasn't coming. He just couldn't face the wailing at the moment. He'd tell her closer to fall, when school started and she was more distracted, although he wasn't sure how that would work since she didn't have anything to do with school. In fact, as far as he could see, Chickie's problem was that she didn't have anything to do at all.

Linc did. He hired a plumber to come in and fix the plumbing, and an electrician to come in and fix the wiring, and painters to paint the outside of the house ("Yellow with blue and white trim," Chickie told him, "because that's what Daisy would want," and he went along with it because it was easier than arguing or explaining that Daisy was no longer in the picture), but he hunkered down to do everything else, drawing on the years he'd spent trying to keep his mother's house from falling apart until there was enough money to move her to a better one. The irony occurred to him as he was sanding down a spackled patch: he'd finally gotten his two brothers through college and they had enough money to move her to a new home, but she'd refused to go. So he was still going back to Sidney—patching new cracks as they appeared, repainting and refinishing—only now in a giant leap forward, he had *two* old houses to keep going. That was not part of his plan at all, and it was all because of women: his mother who wouldn't move, Chickie who had picked this house, and Daisy, who had inspired it.

The worst part was that Chickie was right; Daisy would have loved the house. As he worked patching and painting the walls, he could see her trailing her long skirts across the gleaming living room floor, dropping that awful hat in the high-ceilinged hall, shooting him that smile from the arched doorway into the kitchen, sitting on the solid oak stairs and explaining the world to him through the ornate railing. Once he found himself holding an imaginary argument with her as he painted, convincing her that it was practical to paint all the walls white. The really irritating thing about that hadn't so much been that he caught himself doing it as it was that she'd been winning. Chickie didn't help; she dropped by regularly with notes about curtains and rugs and the best place to buy bread, all beginning "Dear Daisy." And it was his fault; he'd started it with that first dumb story he'd told about his fiancée. Everything Daisy had said about stories came back to him: the stories you told were unreal but not untrue; she wasn't really there, but she was everywhere.

He sighed and kept on painting, and when he moved his chrome and leather furniture into the big old rooms, he knew what Daisy would say, and he had a feeling she was right, so it was a damn good thing she wasn't there to say it.

"Linc moved out yesterday," Julia told Daisy early in June.

"I know." Daisy nodded toward a huge vase of gladioli, birds of paradise, and cattails sitting on the wobbly table near her door. "He sent me flowers."

Julia squinted at the arrangement. "Obviously chosen with you in mind, I don't think. Didn't he get to know you at all in Prescott?"

"No." Daisy tried to keep the melancholy out of her voice. "He didn't want to. I think I made his teeth hurt."

"Oh?" Julia shot her one of those Hello? glances. "Well, he's not exactly your type either, is he?"

"No." The melancholy was there for sure, and

Daisy gave up. "He makes me crazy, if you want to know the truth. I mean, he's just like my father, all orders and rules."

"But . . ." Julia prompted.

"But I felt really good with him," Daisy finished. "I felt safe. And he's not exactly like my father. He never made me feel guilty or beholden or—well, okay, he did make me feel clueless, but not on purpose. Even though we were surrounded by all those people and telling that big story, I felt safe." She met Julia's eyes. "I don't think I've ever felt safe, not since I caught on that my mother's grip on reality wasn't a good one. And I must have been about four, so it's been a while."

Julia scrunched farther down in Daisy's old flowered armchair, staring into space as she thought. "You're right about Linc, but I think that's what I *didn't* like about him when I was with him. No challenge, no excitement. As long as Linc is around, nothing goes wrong."

"Yeah." Daisy thought about riding through the night beside Linc in his awful car, wrapped in darkness and safety. "I loved that."

"Just that?"

Well, no. There was his body. Daisy stood up and went to the kitchen to distract herself. "Just that. Do you want some coffee?"

"I'd rather have the truth."

Daisy exhaled loudly and turned back to her. "Okay, it was not just that. I was tempted by his body. Really, really tempted. I'm still dreaming about him. But that body is attached to a mind that thinks I'm a nightmare, and I couldn't stand the constant disapproval even if he wanted to take me to Prescott, which he doesn't, since he won't even talk to me in the hall, and now he's gone, so it's not an issue, so do you want coffee?" She blinked hard and realized there were tears coming, so she turned and went to the kitchen without waiting for Julia's answer.

It was just as well. Julia went for the jugular. "Would you have gone to Prescott if he'd asked?"

Daisy took a coffee cup down from the shelf and shut the cabinet door carefully. "I don't know. Maybe." She turned and waved her hand at her apartment. "This isn't working for me. I need to reinvent myself if I'm going to grow as an artist. I can't hold on to the past, and I can't keep doing the same things. But it's so hard here, always scrambling for money and trying to convince myself I'm good even though nobody else thinks so—"

"I think so."

"—and now even just painting is hard." Daisy slumped against the counter and tried to put into words the realization that had been growing in the back of her mind during the past year. "I'm stuck in the old me, and I don't know how to get out. I just know the old me isn't the real me anymore."

"And Prescott would have made you reinvent yourself." Julia nodded. "Well, sure, but it would have made you reinvent yourself into a lie."

"Maybe not." Daisy closed her eyes and pictured herself in Prescott in that little Victorian house, something that was pretty easy since she'd been doing it ever since she and Chickie had first driven down Tacoma Street. "The college is conservative, but the town isn't. There was an art gallery. And a house, a really, really darling house, not an apartment. Maybe I could have reinvented myself into something real there." The coffeemaker sputtered, and Prescott in the spring vanished back into her apartment: cluttered, stale, and everything her life was that she didn't want it to be. "But it wouldn't have worked, and it's probably just a cop-out anyway."

"Maybe not," Julia said. "Linc's a good guy. Maybe it would have worked."

"Not in a million years," Daisy said. "Now, do you want coffee or not?"

Julia took the coffee and tried to keep the conversation about Linc going, but Daisy had had enough. She stonewalled until Julia gave up in exasperation and left, which was no improvement since that gave Daisy more time to think about Prescott and Linc, which made her breathe a little faster, which made her angry. *Stop it,* she told herself. *Especially stop thinking about how nice and solid he was with his arms around you and how gorgeous he looks with his shirt off. He's probably sleeping with Little Gertrude by now, the incestuous jerk.*

That thought was a killer, and Daisy shoved Linc firmly out of her mind, telling herself that the last thing she needed in her life was another disapproving male, but as the summer wore on, it got harder and harder to paint, and she began to hate her apartment, feeling as if she were trapped in it with the corpse of her old life. Sometimes then, in the middle of the night, Linc would creep back into her thoughts, and she'd think, *He wasn't disapproving when he had his arms around me.* And then she'd kick herself and try to forget him again.

In September, Linc went to Crawford's office for an early morning meeting to discuss the curriculum committee he had been assigned to, but the first thing Crawford said when Linc was sitting across from him was "When's Daisy coming? Chickie's driving me crazy, asking every day. What's the hold up?"

Linc took a deep breath and dropped the bomb. "She's not coming, sir. We had some problems over the summer, and we've decided it's best to just go our separate ways." It sounded lame and rehearsed, so he tried to look miserable, as if he missed Daisy dreadfully. When he thought about her, it wasn't that hard. Those imaginary conversations were taking their toll.

"What?" Crawford leaned across his desk, glowering.

"It was just one of those things, sir." Linc shrugged. "She wasn't ready to get married. I lost her."

Crawford thumped the desk. "Well, get her back, boy. A woman like that is one in a million." Crawford leaned away and hooked his thumbs in his vest. "You bring her back and marry her here. Chickie wants to do the wedding in our backyard." Crawford got a faraway smile on his face. It was ugly. "Daisy loved the gazebo, you know."

This was bad. Chickie was obviously not the only one fantasizing about Daisy. "Yes, sir, she did, but I don't think—"

Crawford shot him another slashing glare. "You sure don't, boy, or you'd never have let her go. Now, you get out of here this afternoon. You want to fly? I'll have Millie make your reservations. One going out and two coming back." He pressed down on the intercom button. "Millie!"

"Uh," Linc began, and Crawford glowered at him again and told his secretary to make plane reservations. He kept on glowering through the next ten minutes of Linc's increasingly frantic explanations as to why bringing Daisy back was impractical, implausible, and impossible, until his secretary interrupted them with the ticket information.

"One out and two back, Dayton International at eleven," she said, handing a memo with the ticket numbers to Linc. "Have a nice flight."

Crawford glared at him. "*Go.*"

Booker found Linc standing in the hall, trying to figure out what to do next. "You look like a man who needs a drink." Booker took his arm. "Come on."

Linc opened his mouth to argue and then realized that Booker hadn't said three words to him all summer. If he was offering a drink now, there was an agenda involved, so he shut up and followed the little man to his office.

Booker waved him to a chair and took a bottle from his bottom drawer. "How about Scotch."

"Yeah. Sure." Linc sank into the chair. "And a syringe."

"Straight into the vein, is it?" Booker chuckled. "Well, I can't say as I blame you. You've really got yourself in a mess." He pulled two glasses out of the same drawer and kicked it shut with his shin.

Linc stopped thinking about how miserable he was. "How'd you know? I just got out of Crawford's office."

Booker pursed his lips and looked up at the ceiling. "Let me guess. You told him your engagement has been broken off, and he's now sending you back to get—what's her name—Rosie."

"Daisy."

"Daisy." Booker nodded and poured. "Only you can't, because you were never engaged to her in the first place." He held out one of the glasses to Linc as he sat down in his desk chair.

Linc blinked once at him and took the glass from him. "How long have you known about Daisy?"

"Since the first interview." Booker drank some Scotch, savoring it. "I asked you if you were married, and you said no, and Crawford had a heart attack, and I watched your fiancée born right before my eyes." He looked at Linc over his horn-rimmed glasses. "You were pretty good, actually."

Oh, yeah. So good Booker had nailed him at the beginning. Linc sighed. "Why didn't you tell Crawford?"

"Because I wanted to hire you." Booker set his glass down, exasperated. "I wanted a good teacher in the department, someone with research experience.

Your publication is sterling and your teaching evaluations are even better. And you're working on a new book, aren't you?"

Linc gave up being surprised. "Yes. How'd you know?"

Booker shrugged. "Anybody we hired, I was going to have to live with for a long time. I looked into you."

Linc went back to the obvious. "Then you knew I wasn't engaged when you asked me."

"I hadn't heard about a fiancée, but I wasn't asking about one either. I don't give a damn whether you're married or not. That's Crawford's question. I just asked you about it because it makes him happy."

"You must have really enjoyed the weekend we spent here." Linc tried to remember how Booker had reacted.

"Almost as much as I enjoyed hearing what your book was about. Nineteenth-century birth control as subversive feminism. Crawford's going to have a coronary when he finds out." Booker laughed. "I'm going to enjoy that."

Linc thought about getting annoyed and decided it wasn't worth it. "Not if I'm not here to write it."

Booker waved that off. "You'll be here. You signed a contract. And Crawford will forgive all when you get what's-her-name, Daisy, back here."

Nobody was listening to him. "What's-her-name isn't coming back here."

"You won't make full professor without her." Booker leaned back in his chair. "Crawford likes faculty wives. Especially attractive faculty wives. And he has grave suspicions about single men in their thirties."

Linc rolled his eyes.

"I know," Booker said. He stretched out his hand and snagged the bottle again. "I told you, he's a fool. But he's a powerful fool. Get her back."

Suppose she did come back... Linc sipped his Scotch and let himself openly consider the idea for the first time, hating how much he liked it. There were many good reasons why the whole thing was a bad idea, reasons that mainly featured Daisy's mouth and Daisy's body, but the truth was, he missed her. He wanted to show her Prescott and the house and watch her face and see her smile and—

Booker picked up the phone. "I'll call you a cab."

Daisy carefully painted in the tiny pink dress that made Rosa Parks stand out like a beacon on the crowded bus. She moved the brush back to the china plate she was using as a palette and picked up a deeper rose to paint in the pleats in Rosa's skirt, and then she stopped and sighed. Liz twitched an ear at her sigh, and Annie jerked her head around, but nothing else changed. Daisy stared at the painting, one she really believed in, one she really wanted to do, one she really didn't want to do. Part of her genius was her attention to detail, but it was the part of her genius that was starting to make her nuts. She suddenly wanted to paint Rosa large, in big, juicy slashes of paint, but that would have been ridiculous. She couldn't tell detailed stories in big, juicy slashes, and stories were her life. Except she didn't like her life anymore. *I need a change,* she cried silently, but it was the same old cry and there was no change coming, so she took a deep breath and painted the first pleat.

Then she heard the outer door slam shut, and seconds later somebody pounded on her door.

Liz and Annie both looked at her. "Maybe this is it," she said to them. "Maybe we're getting a new life." She put down her brush and went to answer the knock.

He was thinner than she remembered, but he had the same handsome face, the same tapering hips, the same stereo he'd stolen from her months before. "I don't believe this," she said, and slumped against the doorframe. "Derek, what are you doing here?"

"Hello, baby." Derek beamed at her and held up

the stereo with the two small speakers stacked on top. "I brought you this."

"Thank you." Daisy took the stereo stack from him. "Now, good-bye," she said, and tried to shut the door with her hip.

Derek blocked it with his foot. "That's all? No, Derek, sweetheart, honey, baby, I missed you? No, God, it's good to see you? No, come on in and take off your clothes?"

"No." Daisy was still trying to close the door. "I'm trying to move in a new direction, not backtrack. Go away." She gave up on the door and went to put the stereo down, and when she turned around, he was in the apartment, looking winsome and contrite and truly annoying.

"I want to come back, Daisy," he said with all the fake sincerity he was capable of.

And I had a relationship with this? Daisy mentally kicked herself and then moved on. "I don't want you back, Derek. The stereo is still welcome, of course, but you're not. Go away."

"You're a hard woman, Daisy." Derek grinned at her and kicked the door closed behind him. "That's one of the million things I loved about you." He opened his arms to her. "Come on, you don't mean it."

"Sure, I do." Daisy detoured around him and opened the door again. "Get out. I'm not interested."

Derek leaned toward her, obviously ready to deal the ace up his sleeve. "Daisy, the band cut a record. I'm going to be rich." He stood back to enjoy her reaction.

Daisy shook her head. "I can't afford you until you're rich. Get out."

Derek was, as always, a slow learner. And of course there was that hearing problem. "Just a place to stay for a while, love."

"No. Get out."

"Daisy, baby. Did you forget this?" He reached for her and wrapped his arms around her and kissed her neck while she shrank away.

"Let *go*." Daisy fell into the hall with him as she tried to squirm out of his grasp. Derek was no rapist, but he was a twit and there was a limit to how much of this she was going to put up with. She kicked him hard on the shin, and as he gasped, she heard the front door open. "Help!" she called out, hoping Derek would give up since they had an audience.

Derek didn't have time. Seconds later he was sprawled across the hall.

Daisy straightened her sweater and turned to her rescuer. "Thank you. He wasn't actually—" Her voice faded away.

Linc loomed over Daisy, supporting himself with one hand on her doorframe as he tried to bring order and logic into her life again. The three Scotches he'd had on the plane to get his nerve up had joined the drink that Booker had given him, and now it felt right that he should be lecturing her. "*Never* open your door to anyone you don't know."

"She knows me," the creep who'd attacked her said from the floor. "I'm her boyfriend. Who the hell are you?"

Her boyfriend? Linc focused on him. Oh, right. The musician. Darrin or Derek or something. Well, he was history. "I'm her husband." Linc turned and loomed over him too. "Go away or I'll break your fingers."

"You got married?" Derek stared at Daisy, indignant. "I was only gone eight months."

"But you never wrote," Daisy pointed out. "So I took the next guy who asked. He's a hit man. He makes sure that the people who bother me disappear. In fact—"

Linc watched her get into her story. It made him feel nostalgic and dizzy, and he put a hand back on the wall to steady himself. Daisy's eyes widened and she picked up speed. "He knows my brother in New

Jersey. So you have to go now." She took Linc's hand
and he squeezed hers, glad to feel her warm beside
him as she tugged him through the doorway.

"You don't have a brother in New Jersey." Derek
picked himself up from the floor. "You're an only
child from Tennessee."

Daisy was supporting a lot of Linc's weight now;
she was stronger than he'd thought. "He's adopted.
Thanks again for the stereo. Now, go away or...my
husband will hurt you." She looked up at Linc.

"Yeah." Linc nodded slowly. "I could do that."

"Come on, honey." Daisy nudged him with her
hip, and he stumbled into the apartment so she could
slam the door behind them.

"What was he doing here?" Linc squinted at her.

"He wants me back." Daisy put her hands on her
hips. She still had great hips. "I'm unforgettable. I
thought you moved."

Oh, hell, now he had to explain things. "I did.
Look, do you have any coffee? I don't feel very well."

Daisy hesitated and then said, "Sure," and moved
toward the kitchen while he watched her, thinking
unsafe thoughts.

This is a very bad idea, he told himself, and then he
followed her.

• • •

Daisy was out of coffee, but there was some left over from the day before in the pot, so she microwaved it, watching him out of the corner of her eye while she worked. He was as big and solid as she remembered. And still square-jawed handsome. And safe. Oh, damn. She took the cup from the microwave when it dinged and put it in front of him.

He drank from it and made a face.

"Sorry, that's all I have."

"No, no, it's fine." He focused on her, and his face looked funny. Then he took a deep breath, flaring his nostrils, and looked better.

Tense, Daisy thought.

"You remember the Cinderella deal?" She nodded and he said, "I need a wife."

Daisy's heart kicked up speed, but she kept her face calm. "That's what you needed before."

"No." Linc shook his head, and the momentum kept him shaking seconds longer than necessary. "Before I needed a fake fiancée. Now Crawford wants me to get married in his garden. He wants me to marry you."

Daisy sat down. Marriage. For a moment she'd almost thought her story was going to come true, that he was going to invite her back to be a fake fiancée for a while, but this was the real thing, and standing up in front of a minister and lying to God was not a possibility. "Didn't you tell him we had irreconcilable differences?"

"Yeah. He told me to reconcile them." Linc waved that away. "Forget that." He leaned forward and presented his sentences carefully to her. "The house I've got has four bedrooms. You could set up your studio in one and paint all day. I'll support you. All you have to do is show up at campus functions and be a wife. That's all. You don't have to do anything else in Prescott that you're not doing here." He frowned over what he'd said, nodded to himself, pulled his cup back, drank some more coffee, and winced. "I'll make the coffee though."

Daisy tried to think rationally. It wasn't her strong point at the best of times, and it was even worse with Linc sitting across from her in the all too attractive flesh, so she concentrated on the basics. "Let me get this straight. Essentially, you want me to marry you for your money. As God is your witness, if I marry you, I'll never be hungry again?"

Linc thought about it. "That pretty much covers it."

No, it didn't. *You probably haven't noticed, but I have this thing for your body,* she told him silently. She took a deep breath. "What about sex?"

• • •

Linc blinked at her. Her dark hair tumbled over her shoulders and he wanted to tangle his fingers in it and pull her toward him. That was a bad idea, which was a shame because it had tremendous appeal. "I told you, you don't have to do anything in Prescott that you're not doing here." *Unless you want to,* he thought, looking at her big brown eyes glowing at him. *I want to.*

Daisy folded her arms and leaned back, and it was just his bad luck that she folded them under her breasts, and there went his mind again. "What are you going to do for sex?" she asked him.

He needed a different topic fast. "That's my problem, and I'll solve it. Don't worry about it."

"You'd cheat on me? What would Crawford say?"

Linc thought of Crawford and his faculty wives. "He'd probably say 'Way to go, son.' College professors are not known for their fidelity."

She stuck out her chin at him, and his gaze traveled down the curve of her throat.

"What about me?" she asked.

"You? Sex?" He hadn't thought about her having an affair. Or, rather he had thought about it, but he had thought about her with him. Some other guy? He didn't like it, but he couldn't afford to scare her off. He shrugged. "Be discreet."

"Sure, that's always been one of my specialties."

She took a deep breath. "You know, I'm not sure I wouldn't like to pretend to be married for a while. I can't do it for real, the vow would be a lie to God, but I think I could pretend. It sounds sort of . . . secure."

He nodded, nudging her down the road to Prescott. "Security I can give you. And we could get married by a judge. No God in the ceremony at all."

She thought about it. "When's midnight?"

"Midnight?"

"You know. When Cinderella turns back into a pumpkin. Midnight. When we stop being married."

"Oh." Linc hadn't thought far enough ahead to worry about an end. "I don't know."

Daisy pursed her lips. She had great lips. Forget her lips. "A year? Lots of marriages hit the skids after a year. Or maybe the end of the school year. June. That's ten months. I'll flounce off at the end of June and leave you to be consoled by your adoring students and Little Gertrude."

"Ten months is fine. Whatever." He was having trouble focusing again. "Will you do it?" He suddenly straightened and patted his jacket pocket. "Wait a minute. Let me do this right." He pulled out the daisy ring they'd used the last time they were in Prescott and offered it to her, and for some reason, his hand shook. He took a deep breath. "Daisy Blaise, will you marry me?"

Daisy felt her throat catch as she looked at her old ring, the tiny sapphire blinking in the lamplight. It was pretty and sweet, the kind of ring Daisy Blaise would love. Linc had been right to insist on it. Daisy Flattery still liked the chased silver and free-form pearls, but Daisy Blaise would want this ring. If she put it back on, she'd be Daisy Blaise again; Linc obviously thought she still was; he'd even called her that. If she went along with it, she could have everything she wanted and needed.

It's time for a change, she told herself. *Stop being such a coward.* She nodded at Linc and said "Yes," and he exhaled and slipped the ring on her finger, fumbling a little because her hands were shaking and so were his.

Oh, my God, she thought as she felt her hand in his. *What am I doing?*

Then Linc stood up and said, "Let's get started," and Daisy pulled her hand back.

"Started on what?"

"Calling movers," Linc said. "Packing your clothes." He frowned even as he mentioned her clothes. "We've got to get back to Prescott tonight. Our return flight leaves at seven."

Daisy's jaw dropped. "Tonight?"

"Why wait?"

Daisy looked around the apartment she'd had for eight years. She'd loved it, but now it was too small, like her old life. Just like in the fairy tale: the Prince had come along and swept her out of the ashes, and it would ruin the story if he stopped to pack or cancel the phone. "All right." She stood up. "All right, then. Let's go."

She watched bemused as Linc called the movers, who agreed to come on Wednesday. Then she called Julia, who laughed when she told her she was going to Prescott and promised to take the day off from school to watch the movers, especially when they were packing Daisy's stained glass lamp. Linc left to buy a travel case for the cats, and when he got back, Daisy had her clothes packed and was sitting on the boxes, feeling a little lost.

Linc stood in front of her, looking efficient and in charge and that didn't help her qualms any. "Our return flight is in two hours," he told her. "I picked up tranquilizers for the cats. See if you can find Annie." He looked at Liz sprawled out on the floor, asleep in the sun. "I have enough for two in case Liz regains consciousness."

"Forget Liz, give them to me," Daisy said.

• • •

Daisy was so stunned when she saw Linc's house that she sat down on the curb to get her breath. It was her house, gleaming yellow in the twilight just the way she'd imagined it. Less than twelve hours earlier she'd been stuck in her old story, and now she'd been given everything she wanted for her new one. It seemed too good to be true, but there was the house in front of her.

Linc paid the cabdriver and then turned and saw her on the curb. "What are you doing?"

"It's perfect," she told him.

"Good," he said. "Now get up off the curb before the neighbors think you're weird."

Daisy thought about telling him where he could put the neighbors but didn't. *This is his story,* she reminded herself as she stood up. Then she looked at the house again, so beautiful in the autumn evening. There was no reason she couldn't make his story part of hers, at least the house part. In a way it already was; he'd painted it yellow for her.

But after the tour of the house, she knew it was still his story and still his house. True, the house did have glowing amber wood floors and an ornate mantel and an oak staircase, but every single wall was painted stark white.

She looked at Linc in despair. "White?"

He frowned at her, defensive. "It looks clean. And neat."

Neat. Something she obviously wasn't. The tension of the past day made her temper spurt. "Are you kidding? We could operate in here. I can't live in a hospital room, Linc. And, my God, this furniture, all this leather and metal stuff. I can't live like this."

He sat down, looking exhausted and pulled the cat carrier toward him. "So you can mix in some of your stuff when the movers send it." He opened the door to the cat carrier and looked inside. "Hello?"

"They're still asleep." Daisy looked around at his black leather and chrome. "I don't think our furniture is going to mix."

"Let's cross that bridge when we come to it." He picked up one of her boxes and started upstairs. "The house is the least of our problems."

Daisy looked around at the white walls and ugly furniture. "No, it isn't," she said. Whether he liked it or not, his furniture was going to have to go and hers would have to come in. She felt her spirits rise at the thought. He'd like it once he saw her things in the house. Her stuff was old-fashioned and warm, just like the house. He'd love it once he saw it. He'd say, "Daisy, it's amazing what color can do for a house. Thank you." And she'd smile and he'd smile and the cats would curl up in the windows and they'd live happily ever after.

Feeling much better, Daisy picked up a box and followed Linc upstairs.

Once he'd helped her unpack and she'd hung her clothes in the empty bedroom across the hall from his, she explored the house, making plans, mentally moving her furniture in and burning his. The moon was high by the time she climbed the stairs again, and Linc was asleep in the only bed.

"Hey." She poked him.

"Mmmphf."

"Hey." She poked him harder.

"What?"

"Shouldn't you be on the couch like a gentleman?"

"I never said I was a gentleman," he said sleepily. "This is a king size. I'm so tired I couldn't find you if I wanted you. Which I don't. Go to sleep."

As a speech, it was a lot more reassuring than flattering, but she was exhausted too, so she knew how he felt. She went across the hall and changed into her nightgown and took her soap and toothbrush into the bathroom. By the time she was ready for bed, he was asleep again.

She crawled in beside him and fell asleep almost instantly, dreaming of gleaming wood floors with Liz sprawled in the sunlight.

Linc woke up the next morning with his arm around Daisy, pressed close against her back. She was wearing the same thin cotton T-shirt she wore the night they'd spent in the motel, but this time they were in the same bed. And he was awake in more ways than one.

SIX

MOVE BEFORE SHE wakes up, he told himself, but he didn't want to. She was so soft and warm and round and he felt so good pressed up against her. It took all the self-control he had not to move his hand up to the fullness of her breast. She'd be terrific to sleep with in the winter, he thought as he moved his cheek against her hair, and then he realized that he wouldn't be sleeping with her in the winter. *She'd be terrific to sleep with anytime,* he thought, growing dizzy with the thought. *Maybe we could . . .*

No. The last thing in the world he needed was to have an affair with a temporary wife. That would simply add an emotional element to an already impossible situation. No, no, no.

So why is your arm still around her? he asked himself.

"Why is your arm around me?" Daisy asked sleepily.

"I never had a teddy bear when I was little." Linc held himself very still. "I'm compensating. Go back to sleep. This is completely asexual."

"I don't think so." Daisy yawned and stretched a little, which compounded Linc's problem. "Is that a gun in your pajamas, or are you just glad to wake up with me?"

He rolled away from her and got up to get dressed. "That's your imagination."

"Right," she said, and fell back asleep.

She had to be the calmest woman in the world. Either that or she trusted him completely. That was depressing somehow. He went to take a cold shower.

After Linc left, Daisy took a cold shower. *Do not think about this man,* she told herself as she shuddered under the icy water. *Do not think about how good he felt wrapped around you. Do not think about how good all that hardness would have felt moving inside you.*

She felt hot in spite of the cold water. *Stop it, Daisy,* she told herself. *He's not the kind of person you want to get involved with. Just marry him and forget him.*

Right.

She plunged into her work, concentrating on unpacking her clothes and answering the phone and planning the house.

Linc called and his voice made her warm again. She listened absently to him telling her that their blood tests were at eleven and that he'd called his mother.

Pansy, she thought guiltily, and then asked, "What did she say?"

"Congratulations."

"That's it?"

"She said she'd try to be here for the wedding."

"Oh." Meeting Linc's mother was probably going to go a long way toward explaining his furniture and his car.

"My brothers are coming," Linc went on. "We'd better make some reservations at the college inn. One for my brothers and one for my mother in case she makes it. Anyone else?"

"Julia. She's driving over on Wednesday. And my mother. I haven't called her yet, but she'll be here."

"Oh, great." He sighed. "At least it'll all be over by Friday."

Daisy looked at the phone in disbelief. No, it wouldn't. That's when it would start. They'd be *married*. The thought galvanized her into action and she called her mother.

"Mom, this is Daisy."

"How are you, baby?" Her mother's voice was vague as usual, and Daisy pictured her staring into space, trying to concentrate.

"I'm getting married, Mom."

Pansy's voice sharpened considerably. "What? To who? Since when? I don't understand."

Daisy took a deep breath and plunged into her mother's questions. "He's a wonderful man, Mom. A college professor. He just swept me off my feet. We're getting married Thursday here in Prescott, Ohio."

"Where?" Pansy's voice rose to a squeak. "What's going on?"

"I'm marrying Lincoln Blaise in Prescott, Ohio, on Thursday," Daisy repeated. "Can you come?"

"Can I come? What are you talking about? Of course I can come. Oh, Daisy, are you sure?"

Not at all, she wanted to say, but instead she said, "I'm positive, Mom. Let me give you the address and phone number." Daisy repeated it twice while Pansy dithered on the other end of the line.

"Oh, dear," Pansy said finally. "Are you sure? Oh, Daisy. Let me call you back."

There was a dial tone suddenly, and Daisy blinked at the phone. What could her mother possibly be doing?

Half an hour later, as Daisy was going out the door to meet Linc for the blood tests, the phone rang again.

"I found Prescott on the map," Pansy said. "It's near Dayton. I'm flying in this afternoon at one-fifteen, so you come pick me up, and then we can talk."

"This afternoon." Daisy closed her eyes. "You bet, Mom. This afternoon."

Chickie called a minute later, catching her again on her way out the door, to tell her that they had a judge lined up for Thursday, and that they needed to order a cake and a dress.

"Let's do the dresses this afternoon." Chickie's voice came over the phone vivid with excitement. "We'll drive to Dayton and pick them out and then we can make sure the cake and the napkins coordinate."

"Dresses? Coordinate?" Daisy sat down on the floor.

"How many bridesmaids are you having?"

"Bridesmaids?"

"Oh, honey . . ."

"One." Julia was going to drive in for the wedding anyway. She might as well participate.

"Size?"

"Small," Daisy said, thinking she'd look like a giantess at her own wedding.

"I'll pick you up at twelve. We can have lunch first. Is that okay with you, honey?"

"Make it twelve-thirty," Daisy said. "I've got blood tests right now and the bank. And we might have to have lunch at the airport because I'm picking my mother up at one-fifteen."

"Oh, good," Chickie said, but she didn't sound enthusiastic.

Daisy headed for the door and the phone rang again. She picked it up prepared to tell Linc she was on her way, but a woman answered.

"This is Gertrude Blaise." Linc's mother had a voice like unrisen bread.

Daisy heard herself chirping to compensate for the deadness on the other end of the line. "Mrs. Blaise. How nice—"

"I am driving down today but I am not sure of the location of the campus. Could you please arrange for Lincoln to meet me at the Dayton airport at one o'clock? He is not answering his office phone."

She heard the front door open and turned to see Linc coming in.

"Daisy, we're late—" he began, and she grabbed him by his tie.

"He just came in the door, Mrs. Blaise," she told his mother. "But I'll be able to meet you at the airport. My mother's coming in at the same time. We can all talk."

There was a long silence as Linc looked confused and Gertrude thought things over. "Thank you," she said finally. "That will be most satisfactory." Then she hung up.

Linc peeled her fingers off his neckwear. "What's going on?"

Daisy looked at him with undisguised distaste. She was going to spend the Afternoon in Hell while he went out to the college and taught people who couldn't talk back if they wanted to graduate. "Your mother and my mother are both coming into Dayton this afternoon. Chickie and I will be picking them up, and then we're going to buy a wedding dress and order a cake. All of us. Together." She folded her arms and looked at him.

"I'll make it up to you somehow." Linc's eyes were full of sympathy. "I don't know how, but I'll find a way."

The phone rang again. "We have given that number to too many people," Daisy told him, and went to get her purse while he answered it. When she came back, he said, "The movers aren't bringing your furniture until Thursday."

"I'm getting married Thursday."

"So am I. Maybe we can make them ushers."

Linc's mother wasn't hard to spot at the airport; she looked just like her son. Tall and broad with dark eyes and iron-gray hair that must have once been black like Linc's, she looked like the kind of woman who would raise repressed sons. She looked like a prison warden right before the big break, sensing the tension in the air. She looked like Linc when he was being a pain in the butt.

"I'm Daisy." Daisy walked up to her and extended her hand. "And I'm just so pleased—"

"Thank you for meeting me." Gertrude did not extend her hand, so Daisy transferred the gesture into a wave toward Chickie.

"And this is Chickie Crawford. She's having the wedding and the reception for us in her garden."

"We just love your son." Chickie grabbed for the hand that Daisy hadn't captured. "Linc is just the sweetest thing."

She exhaled a lot of gin, and Gertrude looked at her with distaste. "Thank you. I am parked in the short-term parking lot, so if we could go to the hotel now..."

"Oh, no," Chickie said gaily. "We're going to pick out Daisy's dress first."

"I have to get over to gate thirty-one." Daisy backed away. "I'm late. My mother—"

"We'll be right behind you, honey," Chickie said, and Daisy left the two women together and ran for the other gate, where she found Pansy pacing and checking her watch.

"Oh, Daisy!" Pansy fell on her and cried, her fluffy yellow curls bobbing with her sobs. "My baby."

"Easy, Mom. I'm all right."

"You're getting married." Pansy hung on Daisy, looking up from her five feet two inches at the giant of a daughter she'd borne.

"You're going to love him, Mom. He's a nasty-looking Yankee. A carpetbagger if I ever saw one."

"Did he just sweep you off your feet?" Pansy had pulled back and was clasping Daisy's shoulders, looking up into her eyes. "Do you just love him to death?"

"Absolutely," Daisy said, and stopped when she realized she sounded like Linc. She waved her ring hand at her mother. "Isn't my ring cute?"

"He got you pearls," Pansy said in a flat voice. "Why not diamonds?"

Oh, boy. "Because I wouldn't wear diamonds. He gave me my own checking account to do whatever I want with. And he wants me to paint full-time. He calls me Magnolia. And"—Daisy searched desperately for something else that was true that would make Linc look good—"and he's never been married before. And he bought me this darling little Victorian house and told me I can decorate it any way I want, and—"

"Oh, Daisy, he sounds wonderful." Pansy began to cry again.

Good, Daisy thought, *because I was running out of things to say. I was down to the Nazi car and furniture, and that would have been bad.*

"Yoo-hoo!"

"And this is Chickie and Gertrude!" Daisy made the introductions as cheerily as possible. Gertrude took being called by her first name fairly well for a prison warden. Chickie and Pansy sized each other up, two southern belles not happy to share the charm sweepstakes.

"Gotta get my dress!" Daisy swept them all off to the car, cursing Linc, who was safe in Prescott.

"Now, for your flowers I think you should have roses," Chickie said as they drove down the interstate. "Pink roses."

"Roses? Do you think so, Chickie?" Pansy's voice was sweet from the backseat. "It just seems like everyone has roses. How about lilies, honey?"

"Lilies?" Daisy turned to look at her mother in the back beside Gertrude. "I thought lilies were for funerals."

"No, no." Pansy turned her little nose up. "Lilies are elegant."

"Carnations are inexpensive and hold their bloom for a reasonable amount of time," Gertrude said.

Oh, no, Daisy thought. *Don't let this be happening.* "Daisies," she said. "I want daisies."

"Oh, honey, no," Pansy began, but Daisy cut her off.

"Linc wants me to have daisies."

"Oh, well, then." Pansy sounded doubtful. "Maybe with some baby's breath..."

"And a few pink rosebuds..." Chickie agreed.

"And some baby carnations," Daisy said to appease Gertrude. "Why don't we wait until we get the dress?"

"Well, I'm sure we can agree on the cake." Chickie looked over at Daisy. "White, of course."

"But men always like chocolate," Pansy protested. "Wouldn't Linc like chocolate, Daisy?"

"Linc doesn't like sweets," Daisy said.

"Lincoln used to like walnut cake," Gertrude said. "He was quite fond of it."

"Pumpkin cake," Daisy said desperately. "Pumpkin cake with walnuts and cream cheese icing."

"Pumpkin cake?" Chickie said, puzzled.

"Pumpkin cake?" Pansy said, shocked.

Gertrude didn't say anything, perhaps because of the walnuts.

"It's a ... private joke," Daisy said weakly. "Like Cinderella. Linc would like it."

"Oh, well, then." Pansy still sounded doubtful.

"Well, your colors can still be pink and white," Chickie said.

"Blue and white," Pansy said.

"Yellow and white," Gertrude said. "Lincoln likes yellow."

Well, at least his mother's showing some animation, Daisy thought. *If they get to kicking and screaming and pulling hair, my money's on her.* She smiled at all three women as impartially as possible, the way she knew Daisy Blaise would smile.

Daisy Flattery would have jumped out of the car and run for it.

Linc came down the stairs when he heard her come in. "How bad was it?"

Daisy dropped her bags on the floor and glared at him. "You owe me."

He winced. "I knew it."

"You never told me you liked walnut cake."

Linc frowned at her. "I hate walnut cake."

"Your mother says you like walnut cake."

"What?" Linc looked shocked. "My mother never let us eat cake. Walnut cake?"

"She also thinks my flowers should be carnations, my dress should be polyester, and our color for the wedding should be yellow."

"My mother said all that?" Linc ran his hand through his hair. "My mother?"

Daisy sat down beside him, too tired to be mad anymore. "We're all eating together at the inn tonight." She leaned against him, grateful for his shoulder. "Make reservations for six."

Linc stiffened. "Six?"

"The Crawfords, Pansy, Gertrude, and us."

"I'm sorry I lied, God." Linc looked up at the ceiling. "I'm sorry I tried to pass this woman off as my fiancée last spring. Please stop punishing me."

Daisy went on brightly, in her best idiot voice. "And then we'll do this again at Thanksgiving and Christmas. And Easter, if we're still married."

"Pumpkin cake." Linc stood, bumping her off his shoulder, and went to make the reservations.

• • •

They survived dinner.

On the bad side, Chickie got drunk, as usual, and Crawford made a pass at Pansy, and Gertrude left before dessert to go back to her room and sleep.

On the good side, nobody insulted anyone blatantly, Pansy thought Linc was wonderful, and Gertrude didn't pull her son aside and tell him to get rid of the crazy brunette.

All in all, Daisy thought as she sat in bed making a list of things to do for the wedding, they'd gotten through it. Now only two more days until the wedding, and all these people would go home.

Linc came into the bedroom wearing sweatpants and nothing else and Daisy lost her breath. He had a beautiful body, firm and muscled without being muscle bound. *I want to draw him,* Daisy thought. *I want to paint him. The hell with that, I want to—*

"Where'd we get those lamps?" Linc pointed to the ginger jars on each side of his high-tech chrome bed frame.

Daisy found her voice. "Chickie's wedding present."

"They're yellow."

Right. He didn't like color. Her lust faded a little. "I don't think ginger jars come in black leather. I'll move them when my furniture comes."

He got into bed beside her. "Yellow." He opened his book.

Daisy looked at his shoulders. *Say something,* she told herself. *Say something fast before you lean over and bite him.* "My mother loves you."

"I know," he said, reading. "She told me."

"Aren't you glad?"

"Yes," he said from his book. "My mother likes you too."

Gertrude? "How can you tell?"

"She spoke to you."

He was so close and he wasn't paying any attention to her and it was all she could do to breathe. Daisy put her hand on his book, and he looked up.

"I'm glad she likes me. She's really very nice. She bought me long underwear today because she said it gets cold in Ohio in the winter. She bought you some too."

Linc's face was blank. "Long underwear."

"It's really sweet, Linc. She wanted us to be warm."

"You're warm enough for both of us." Linc went back to his book. "I like it better cold."

Well, that was in character. Daisy sighed and gave up and went back to her list.

"Did you get the rings?"

"What rings?"

"Wedding bands."

"Oh." Linc frowned. "Why don't you go get one that will go with your ring? You can get the right size that way too."

"What about yours?"

"Mine?"

Daisy looked at him, exasperated. "Not planning on wearing a ring?" she said, and for some reason Caroline sprang into her mind.

"Well, no."

"It's traditional," she said, investing the words with enough weight so that he could translate them into *You'd better*.

Linc did what he'd been trying to avoid doing ever since he'd walked into the bedroom: he looked at Daisy, propped on the pillows beside him. The thin cotton T-shirt was pulled over her breasts by the weight of the covers, and her curls gleamed in the lamplight and her eyes were huge, and he clenched his hands into fists on his book to keep from reaching for her.

That's not all that's traditional, he thought. *If I wear a wedding ring, do I get a wedding night?*

Then another thought chased that one away: *Are you out of your mind?*

"Maybe I'll sleep on the couch." He got out of bed. *Make a note to stay out of beds with Daisy,* he told himself. *A big note.*

"What did I say?" Daisy asked.

"Nothing. We'll go get rings tomorrow. I'll pick you up at eleven again. Good night." He gave himself one more glance at her where she sat warm and round and glowing in the lamplight and then he bolted from the room.

Daisy spent Tuesday trying to organize a wedding with the three witches helping. Chickie and the mothers fought over napkins, centerpieces, vows, showers, favors, appetizers, the bar, the music, and the judge. The only thing they agreed on was that Linc and Daisy should get married, and Daisy wasn't sure Gertrude was behind that one hundred percent.

Tuesday night they had another dinner from hell.

At one point, when Pansy was away from the table, Chickie brought up the question of who was going to give Daisy away.

"Linc said your father's still alive. Don't you think he'd want to give you away?"

"My mother will give me away." Daisy's voice was so tense that even Chickie caught on and didn't mention it again.

Wednesday, Julia drove in and stopped at the house. She looked around and approved. "This is great. I'll have to come back when you've got it done."

"Oh, please do." Daisy sat down on the bottom stair step and started to cry. "I've been so lonely and frazzled and crazed, and everything's been nuts here, and the three mothers are driving me insane, and I haven't even had a chance to paint the walls, let alone a canvas and—"

Julia looked confused. "Three mothers?"

"—and the wedding's tomorrow and that's when my furniture's coming, and you're going to be a bridesmaid and everything's just a mess." Daisy sniffed and looked up at Julia. "I thought this was going to make my life easier."

"Marriage?" Julia shook her head. "You thought wrong. Safer, maybe, more secure, but easier? Nope."

Daisy scowled at her. "Why didn't you mention this before?"

Julia sat down beside her on the stairs. "Because I wanted to be a bridesmaid. Explain the three mothers part to me again."

They managed to get through the rehearsal, the rehearsal dinner, the bachelor party, and the shower without losing their minds, and Daisy woke up at six the morning of her wedding day feeling almost relieved. She listened to Linc clatter down their back steps as he went out to run. *He* would *be an organized fitness nut,* she thought. Running at the crack of dawn. She had nothing in common with this man.

She rolled over and went back to sleep.

Linc left for the college at nine, and Daisy got up and began to move up to the second floor everything chrome that one person could carry. She filled the right front bedroom with Linc's lamps and chairs and bookcases from the living room. Since his desk was already in there, the extra furniture made the room into a study for him. She'd already moved his living room end tables into his bedroom to act as bedside tables. The only things she couldn't move were the awful glass dining room table and the couch. When she was finished, his half of the upstairs was done in black leather and metal. She shuddered and closed the doors.

Then the doorbell rang, and she went to meet the movers.

"The couch goes in here," she told them, sliding open the pocket door to the living room. They brought in her threadbare flowered couch and three mismatched worn brocade chairs. They carried in her collection of miscellaneous chipped and scratched end tables in all sizes and woods. They set her crated paintings behind the couch and rolled her worn Oriental on the floor. They moved Linc's couch and table upstairs to her studio and rolled her big round oak table into the dining room, and the sun came in and highlighted the six unmatched pressed-wood chairs she grouped around it. There was just room enough for the little buffet with the cracked top by the door to the kitchen. They carried her brass bed upstairs and put the mattress on it for her. Her unmatched end tables went into place beside it. They brought up her cheval mirror with the tiny crack, her cedar chest, her dented brass-bound trunk, and her bentwood rocker. Liz checked it all out and then went to sleep in the middle of her bed, satisfied that things were getting back to normal. Annie hid underneath and bitched at the movers with a voice that sounded like breaking glass.

When the movers left, Daisy danced through the house, holding Annie and singing. All this room. All this sun. All her lovely furniture.

She put Annie down and went out to buy flowers for her lovely house.

• • •

When Daisy got back, the Nazimobile was parked in front. "Linc?" she called as she came through the front door.

He erupted from the living room. "What is this?"

"What?" She stepped back, startled.

"All this old"—he waved his hand around wildly—"junk!"

"What junk? These are antiques."

"This stuff has holes in it," he said, incredulous. "The rug, the couch, the chairs. It's junk!"

Daisy felt the familiar tightness come over her; this was her father all over again, making her feel guilty for the things she loved. Well, it wasn't going to work this time. "It's real furniture," she snapped back. "It has personality. It's not that five-and-dime science fiction crud you sit on."

"Five-and-dime?" Linc's eyebrows climbed so high, they almost disappeared into his hair. "That furniture cost me a fortune! It's *designer* furniture."

"Designed by whom?" Daisy crossed her arms and charged. "Darth Vader? The Hitler Youth? You said, the house is yours, Daisy. You said, you're the one spending the most time here, Daisy. You said—"

Linc waved that off. "I know what I said. But I can't have people in here to see this . . . this . . ."

"Careful," Daisy said through her teeth. "I love this, this—"

Linc sat down on the couch and put his head in his hands. "This isn't going to work," he said quietly. "This is not going to work."

Daisy sat down beside him, her back stiff as a ramrod. "I cannot live in a soulless home. That furniture of yours was made by machines for machines," she told him. "I know you're not emotional, I know warmth isn't important to you, but I can't live without light and color and warmth. I can't live with that horrible, horrible, cold, dark furniture."

"All right." He took a deep breath. "But I can't live in squalor." He turned to her, calm but still upset. "Daisy, look at this stuff. It's so worn, you can't see the pattern in the upholstery. The carpet has holes in it. Daisy, it isn't warm, it's worn out."

She looked at the furniture through his eyes, and for the first time it wasn't beautiful to her. She bit her lip as she saw the scratches and chips and holes. He was right. It hadn't mattered when it was just hers. Her friends didn't care about the worn spots and the holes. But his would. Crawford would be horrified. Caroline would sneer. Linc would be embarrassed.

"All right." She fought back her tears, feeling as if she'd lost more than furniture. "But we can't afford new stuff. And I can't afford to throw this stuff out, because when I leave in June, I've got to take it with me."

They stared hopelessly at the furniture together.

"All right," she said again. "Aside from the holes and the faded upholstery, do you have anything against the rest of it?"

"The wood's cracked on most of these tables," he said dully. "The dining room chairs don't match. The dining room table's all right, I guess."

She took a deep breath. "How long do I have to fix this?"

Linc leaned back against the couch. "We're supposed to leave on our honeymoon for four days starting tonight. We'll be back on Monday. The first time we're having guests is after a party at the faculty club next Saturday. The Crawfords, the Bookers, and Caroline and Evan are coming over afterward for drinks."

Daisy nodded, counting days. "Without the honeymoon, that's eight days. We don't need a honeymoon. I can fix this. I've got eight days." She kept nodding. "I can fix this."

"Put your flowers in water first," Linc said quietly.

She looked at the blooms she had forgotten, still clutched in her hand. Daisies for the living room, yellow carnations for the dining room, a bright pink rose for her bedroom.

"You were really happy that your things came,

weren't you?" Linc's voice was gentle. "And I spoiled
it."

"No." Daisy felt ashamed. "You didn't spoil it. I'm
not used to living ... like an adult, I guess. This stuff
is great for me, but it's a disaster for you. I should
have seen it." She met his eyes. "I'm truly sorry."

He put his arm around her shoulders, and they
slumped back into the overstuffed couch together and
stared at their mutual problem.

"Do you really think you can fix it?" He absentmindedly stroked her cheek with his thumb.

Daisy nodded, feeling his thumb move against her
face with each nod. "I can fix anything. I just need to
think."

Cover up the holes, she thought, leaning her cheek
against his hand. That would be a piece of cake. Slipcovers. She'd made slipcovers for Julia last year.
Cracked tables that didn't match could be fixed with
wood putty and paint, though she'd miss the wood.
She could paint it all a bright blue. No. This was for
Linc. She could paint it all white. She could bring out
the detailing in the wood with the major color in the
slipcovers. If she could find flowered fabric, maybe
she could copy some of the flowers on the tabletops.
Or stencil them in a border around the walls.

The more she thought about it, the more enthusiastic she became. It would be like a huge detailed painting, only it would be a house. It could be fun. It really could all work out.

She fought back her rising panic. She could make it work.

Linc watched her, her brow furrowed as she thought. *I've got to be more careful of her,* he thought. One cross word and her world was gone. He hadn't needed to yell the way he had. She wasn't dumb. He'd just been so . . . mad. So embarrassed. She embarrassed him all the time. Maybe that said a lot more about him than it did about her.

He eased his arm out from around her shoulders and gently took the flowers from her grasp. When he took them out to the kitchen to put them in water before he went back to the college, she didn't even notice he left.

If I pick up the pressed-wood detailing in the dining room chairs with the same color, she thought, *I can make them look like a deliberately mismatched set.* She could put seat cushions on them too. And she could stencil the tabletop in the same color. She could make the whole house look like a piece of art.

"I can do this, Linc." She looked for him, but he was gone.

She measured the couch and chairs and then added up the yardage. It was astronomical. Okay, flowers for the couch and one chair. The rest in a nice, cheap solid. And paint. She'd get paint and call Linc and ask him to pick it up on his way home. She could carry the fabric home. No problem.

And then she had to remember to get married tonight too.

She found a bolt of yellow fabric flowered in dusty blue and peach that was marked down. Then she took the fabric to the paint store and matched the colors.

"Two gallons of the peach," she told the boy at the counter, "two of the blue, two of the yellow, and three of glare white. And I need something to fill in cracks in wood tables. I'll be painting over the stuff, so it doesn't matter what it looks like."

"Fine." He finished writing the list and then smiled at her. "Do you want to wait while I mix it?"

"No. My...husband will pick it up later." *My husband,* she thought. *Very strange words.*

The boy wrote up the bill and gave her the total

and she wrote a check, this time for ninety-eight dollars and forty-three cents. With what she'd dropped on the fabric, she was spending more in one day than she used to spend in a month. It was a sobering thought.

"Could you give me your husband's name for the pickup ticket?" the boy asked.

"Linc Blaise. B-l-a-i-s-e."

He looked up. "Dr. Blaise? The history prof out at the college? He's great. I'm Andrew Madden, Mrs. Blaise. I'm one of the students he tutors."

"Hi, Andrew. I'm Daisy." Daisy held out her hand, and Andrew took it and shook it with enthusiasm. "I'll tell him you like his class. He'll be so pleased."

"Oh, don't tell him." Andrew flushed. "He doesn't even know who I am."

"Of course he does," Daisy said, not at all sure that he did.

On the way home she passed the vet's and thought again, absentmindedly, how nice it was that he was close. And then she thought about Andrew.

She'd never heard Linc talk about him. She'd never heard Linc talk about any of his students. Of course, school had been in session only a week, but she'd talked about everybody she'd ever known. Maybe it was just because Linc wasn't a talker. But maybe it was because he didn't get to know his students. She quickly squelched the thought. Linc was a wonderful teacher. Andrew said so. He—

She heard the squeal of brakes and a thump and saw a car go past out of the corner of her eye, and then she saw the dog.

A little skinny black-and-white mutt was lying on its side, moving feebly against the concrete. Daisy dropped her paper-wrapped bolt of fabric and ran to it. Its eyes were dull, and it had stopped moving.

"It's okay," she whispered. "You're okay." She pulled off her sweater and wrapped it around the dog and went to get the bolt. She put the bolt on the pavement and gently lifted the dog onto it as if it were a stretcher. Then she picked it up and carried it back down the block to the vet's.

She banged on the door, and a young man in a white T-shirt and jeans answered it.

"This dog's been hit," she said, out of breath. "Is the vet in?"

"That's me." He opened the screen door.

Daisy followed him into a lab room and put the bolt on a table. She watched the vet examine the dog carefully, concerned and gentle. *What a lovely man,* Daisy thought. What gentle brown eyes. What warmth. You'd need warmth to be a vet. How lucky for this puppy to have this nice man to take care of him.

He looked up and caught her staring at him, and she blushed. He smiled at her.

She leaned forward, anxious about the dog. "Is he going to be all right?"

"When did he lose his eye?"

Daisy felt her heart break with sympathy. "He's only got one eye?"

"Didn't you know?"

"I just met him about a minute ago. Is he going to be all right? He's just a puppy."

"No, he's not," the vet said. "He's more than a year, maybe two."

"He's so little."

The vet nodded. "He's underfed. Probably a stray, since he doesn't have a tag. He'll be bigger when he stands up. He's got legs like stilts, and one of them's broken, so he'll limp for a while. I can splint the leg and keep him for free for a couple of days but ..."

"I'll pay for him." Daisy nodded. "My name's Daisy Blaise, and he's my dog now. Just make him well again."

"Hello, Daisy," the vet said, and held out his hand. "I'm Art Francis."

Daisy took it and shook it with pleasure. "Hello, Dr. Francis."

"No." His eyes were warm on her. "Art."

"Art." She was so happy about the dog that she smiled at him, her full megawatt smile, and he looked lost for a minute.

Daisy stroked the dog's head. "I'll take him home with me when he's ready, but he'll have to make friends with my cats."

"The limp should slow him down and help him get acquainted." Art watched her. "Come in and visit him."

"I will." Daisy leaned close to the dog so he could see her with his good eye. "Every day. Poor little guy."

"Got a name for him? Or should I just write Dog Doe on his card?"

"He needs a powerful name," Daisy said. "Like Hercules." They both looked down at the dog doubtfully. "Or Jupiter. Jupiter is the good luck planet too. Maybe he's my good luck."

Art lifted an eyebrow at her. "A one-eyed crippled dog with a broken tail is good luck?"

Daisy blinked. "His tail's broken too?"

"See that bend in it?"

"Oh, Jupiter, you poor baby." Daisy stroked his head again.

"Jupiter is the perfect name for this dog," Art said. "He just lucked out completely."

"Jupiter." Daisy looked at Art and smiled again.

"Maybe he'll be good luck for me too," Art said. "Come back soon, Daisy."

I should have told him I'm getting married, Daisy thought as she carried the fabric home. Except she wasn't really, not permanently. Only for a year. Ten months. And then...

If she married a vet, she'd have lots of animals. And he was so sweet. And so warm. And he didn't look at her as if she were a disaster in the making.

Tomorrow I'll tell him I'm married, she decided. It was only fair, but when she got home, she sat at the bottom of the stairs and shivered. She shouldn't have been smiling at a vet. She was getting married. In five hours. To a cold man with chrome furniture who was constantly embarrassed by her instead of to someone warm who loved animals. This was wrong.

Julia found her there still shivering half an hour later.

"Daisy?"

"I'm scared," she told Julia. "I'm really, really scared."

Julia nodded. "I would be too. Come on, I have the solution."

Linc stood by the judge and endured a friend of Chickie's who was singing "True Love." Chickie must have picked out the music. Daisy would have chosen something a little more vivid, like "Great Balls of Fire." The music changed and he looked out of the gazebo and down the white carpet that stretched across the Crawfords' lawn.

Julia was walking unsteadily down the carpet with a ring of daisies in her hair, dressed in some sort of gold floaty dress. She looked very cute but very wobbly. *She's drunk,* he thought. Which meant Daisy was too. Julia must have had to get her loaded to get her through this.

He looked past Julia and saw Daisy.

She was wearing white again, and she had daisies in her hair, and a little piece of veil over her eyes. She met his eyes and smiled at him, her megawatt smile loosened a little by alcohol. She looked unstable, and wild, and absolutely enchanting, and her smile made him weak. She stumbled slightly when she got to the steps of the gazebo, and he moved forward and took her elbow to steady her.

"Easy, Magnolia," he whispered.

She looked into his eyes and smiled that smile again. "Hello, love," she said, and he closed his eyes because she was so warm.

"Dearly beloved," the judge began, and Linc concentrated on propping Daisy up through the ceremony. She did very well, but he held on to her tightly anyway in case she suddenly developed a lurch. He knew the people watching probably took it for husbandly devotion. Good for them.

Daisy said her vows clearly, none of which involved lying in front of God, and he slid the ring on her finger.

"You may kiss the bride," the judge said, and Linc looked down into eyes that were full of warmth and love and wine.

He bent and kissed her. She slipped her arms around his neck and pressed herself against him, and his arms went around her to keep her from falling backward and to hold her close. Her lips were so warm and soft that he felt himself drowning in the feel of her mouth on his, and his breath went away. *There are people watching,* he thought, and he let her go. Her eyes were half closed and her mouth was full and open, and he wanted to kiss her again, immediately, again and again.

She opened her eyes and said, "Wow," and he pulled her hand through his arm and walked her back down the aisle while she clung to him.

"That was some kiss," Daisy said breathlessly when they were alone by the rose arbor.

"You're some bride." Linc kissed her forehead, not trusting himself with her mouth. "How much did the two of you have to drink?"

"A bottle of wine. I was a little nervous."

"About me?"

"No!" Daisy looked up at him, her eyes wide. "I know all about you. I just don't know about marriage."

You don't know all about me, he thought. If she did, she wouldn't have married him. Because she didn't know how much he wanted her, and how much he wished he didn't. *Make a note not to kiss Daisy again,* he told himself.

"Congratulations!" Chickie grabbed him and kissed him and then fell on Daisy with glad cries, and the reception started. Gertrude kissed Daisy's cheek and patted Linc on the back, an absolute outburst of emotion for her, and Linc was touched. Pansy wept on everybody. Crawford patted all the women. Julia met Evan York and stayed with him for the whole afternoon, fascinated by his prophecies of doom.

Linc and Daisy just smiled and drank.

Later, the things Linc remembered most about his wedding were Daisy's kiss at the altar, his mother's look of grim approval, and the taste of the pumpkin cake.

It was really very good cake.

SEVEN

BY THE TIME the reception was over, Daisy was so tired and so full of champagne that Linc carried her over the threshold, not because of any tradition but because she couldn't walk. He put her on her bed, threw her quilt over her, and staggered back to his own bed. In the morning he didn't mention the wedding kiss, and neither did she, and they both went to work on their own projects. Linc noticed that Daisy was trying to fix the house, but mostly he worked on his classes, his tutoring, and, wonder of wonders, his book.

"You know," he told Daisy two days after the

wedding, "I wasn't happy that you'd moved all my furniture upstairs, but you were right. That front room makes a nice study. I'm getting a lot done."

"Good." Daisy looked past him, abstracted. "Do you have any objections to a blue dining room?"

"No. What's in the pot on the stove?"

"Vegetable soup. Bread in the bread box. How about a peach living room?"

"Fine." He frowned as what she'd said reached him. "Peach? Oh, fine, I guess. Can I take some soup upstairs while I work?"

Daisy flapped her hand at him while she stared into the dining room. "You can take it anywhere you want. When you meet with your students, will you be using the dining room?"

Linc left her and headed for the kitchen and food. "I'll be using my office at school." He opened the bread box and rummaged to get under the two baked rounds of sourdough and wheat bread Daisy had brought home from the bakery. "Don't we have any real bread?" he called to her.

"That is real bread," she called back. "The packaged stuff you eat is the fake kind. I think you should meet them here at the house. The other profs do. I asked Chickie."

Linc ignored her suggestion because he didn't like

it; the last thing he needed was his professional life slopping over into his personal life. "This stuff isn't even sliced."

"You tear it. Sliced bread is for people with no imagination."

"That's me." He carried his tray through the door. "I'll be in the study."

Daisy spent the eight days after her wedding working on the house, making slipcovers and curtains and painting furniture. She worked until two or three in the morning because she liked working at night, usually getting up at eleven the next morning, two hours after Linc had left for campus. Linc got up at six and ran for an hour, and then came back and worked in the quiet on his book before he left at nine. He was back by five and always in bed by eleven at the latest. They drifted by each other around dinner, checking with each other on concrete topics ("We're out of milk," "Your insurance agent called"), both so absorbed in what they were working on that they barely noticed each other.

Linc told her that he was farther along in his book in eight days than he'd been in eight months. And Daisy had turned a desperation project into a work of art.

She'd unpacked her finished paintings that the movers had stacked behind the couch. Daisy leaned a landscape with a girl dressed in peach against the wall in the living room and put a large blue still life in the dining room and considered them dispassionately. Then she went to work.

She painted the living room pale peach, the hall pale yellow, and the dining room pale blue. She stenciled pale pink and yellow cabbage roses along the ceiling in the living room, and pink cabbage roses along the staircase wall in the hall. Then she free-painted pale blue daisies among the living room roses and white daisies in the hall. The whole effect was muted, faded as if with age. She'd already covered her upholstered furniture—some with the light flowered fabric, some with a coordinating dusty blue—and painted all the wood furniture white, picking out the detailing on the tables with peach and yellow. When the walls were done, she hung flowered draperies from rings on natural wood rods. In the dining room she painted a triple row of white checks along the edge of the ceiling to pick up the blue and white checked tablecloth in her big still life. She hung the still life over her old buffet, now also painted white, the edges trimmed with tiny white and blue checks, and hung blue and white checked curtains at the front windows. The curtains were all lined with white, so the house looked fine from the outside. Daisy was really proud of the linings; a month ago she wouldn't have thought of it, and the house would have looked like a crazy quilt from the street.

Her life was coming together, she thought on Monday night as she wandered through the three rooms she'd finished. The cats had settled in, and Jupiter was coming home tomorrow—she winced as she realized she still hadn't told Linc—and the house had turned into a home. She stopped in the dining room, caught by the realization that they never ate there. Linc either ate while he talked to her, leaning against the kitchen sink, or he took a tray upstairs to the study. Now that the dining room was finished, they could eat like real people. Like Linc's kind of people.

"Look," she said to him when he came down later looking for food. She pulled him out of the kitchen and into the dining room. "You don't need to stand up by the sink anymore."

"It's nice." He looked around, not really seeing anything. "I like standing by the sink. We talk."

He looked lonely standing there, and she wanted to hold him, just go up and put her arms around him and comfort him. *Stop it,* she told herself. He'd just been working too hard. She patted his arm. "We should do more things together. Maybe."

He brightened at the thought. "Run with me tomorrow."

"Run?" Daisy said, appalled.

Linc nodded, suddenly enthusiastic. "You don't get enough exercise. It'll be good for you. Come on, we'll go get you shoes and sweats now. The stores don't close until nine." He picked up his coat.

"Run?" Daisy tried to stall. "I don't know, Linc—"

He was already getting his keys. "Come on." He looked so happy that she followed him out to the car without protest. She'd been thinking more of going to the movies or out for pizza, but she should have known he'd think of something that involved pain and suffering for a good cause. There was a lot of martyr in Linc.

There was a lot of martyr in her too, Daisy thought as she dragged her body out of bed the next morning after only four hours of sleep. The things she'd do to save a fake marriage.

Linc showed her how to warm up and then set off with her at a gentle jog. They fell into a pace in which he would run down a side street, across a block and up the next street to meet her so that he was still getting the workout he was used to but she could keep up. Daisy slowed to a walk every time he got out of sight, trying to keep her heart from exploding. It was on one of these blocks that she met Art coming out of his house to pick up his paper.

"What are you doing?" he asked. "Your face looks like a tomato."

Daisy stopped and tried to breathe. "Jogging. My husband's trying to keep me healthy."

Art frowned. "Does he have a lot of insurance on you? It looks more like he's trying to kill you."

"No, no." Daisy leaned on him for a moment to rest. "This is good for me." She looked up and saw Linc jogging toward them. "Oh, no. I have to run again."

She meant it as a joke, but Art stiffened as he watched Linc run toward them, and she saw Linc through Art's eyes, a big, broad, frowning, dark-haired guy in black sweats.

"He's really nice," she said, and then Linc came up and said "Wimp" to her.

Daisy nodded. "I am. You'll just have to face it. This is Art Francis, the vet."

Linc offered his hand. "Something wrong with Annie or Liz?"

"Annie and Liz?" Art asked.

"Annie and Liz are our cats," Daisy said.

"No," Art said. "I've got Jupiter."

"Jupiter?" Linc asked.

Daisy bit her lip. "A dog got hit by a car."

Linc closed his eyes. "Of course. You would."

"It's a very small dog." Daisy put her hand on his arm, anxious about Jupiter's future. "He won't bother you."

"Daisy, you can have anything you want, including a damaged dog," Linc said, and his exasperation was so clear that Art took a step closer to her. "Can we finish this run now? You really shouldn't stop in the middle of exercise."

"My heart was going to explode." Daisy clutched at him, panting a little. "I would have had a heart attack right here in the street. You would have had to pick up my stiffening body and carry me home, pretending to be grief-stricken, and then you would have had to listen to Chickie, Pansy, and Gertrude fight over the flowers for the funeral and the color of my shroud. Julia would have cracked corpse jokes, Evan would have said that I looked pretty good although, of course, I was dead, and Crawford would have thought about necrophilia. I just did you a big favor by stopping."

Art stared at her, and Linc sighed. "She's not nuts," he said to Art. "She just has these narrative fits where reality recedes."

"I know she's not nuts," Art said shortly, and

turned away from him to talk to Daisy. "Keep coming to the clinic. You're really good at exercising the animals. They like you."

"Oh, good." Daisy beamed at him. "I have so much fun there."

She'd flashed her megawatt without thinking, and Art smiled back, mesmerized. Linc scowled at Art, so she grabbed his arm and tugged him toward the street.

"I'll come by for Jupiter this afternoon," she said to Art. "Come on, Linc. Your pulse rate's dropping."

"Who is that guy?" Linc easily kept pace with her as she ran down the street.

"He's the vet." Daisy puffed hard as she ran. "You know, I think I'm getting the hang of this."

"I don't like the way he looks at you. Stop smiling at him."

"Hey." Daisy frowned as hard as possible while panting her lungs out. "He's my friend."

Linc snorted. "He wants to be more than your friend."

"What do you care?"

"We just got married four days ago. It looks bad."

"Wait a minute." She stopped suddenly, and he had to turn around and jog back to her. "I called the university Friday and you were out for lunch. With Caroline."

"So?"

Daisy put her hands on her hips. Part of the Cinderella deal was that they played fair. "So if you can have lunch with Caroline, I can exercise dogs with Art."

Linc scowled. "It's not the same thing."

"Why not?"

"Because Art wants to exercise a lot more than dogs with you."

"And Caroline doesn't with you?"

Linc waved that away. "That's different."

"Why?"

"Because I'll say no."

"Will you?"

"Yes." He looked insulted. "Hell, yes. We've only been married four days. What kind of creep would I be if I cheated on you already?"

Already? For some reason this conversation was not turning out the way she'd planned. "So when are you planning on cheating? In June?"

Linc turned suddenly wary, as if he'd seen where things were going and didn't like it either. "I don't know. I'm not, I guess. Why are we having this dumb conversation?"

"Because you won't let me exercise the animals at Art's."

"Then go," he snapped. "I don't care. Just stay away from Art."

Daisy stuck her chin out. "I intend to. I have enough problems living with one man who doesn't even notice that I've redecorated the entire downstairs of his house—"

"What?"

"—I don't need to start sleeping with another one."

She took off running down the street, and he watched her before he followed.

She's right, he thought as he steadily gained on her. *What she does is none of my business as long as she's discreet.*

But if he touches her, I'm breaking his fingers.

After Linc left, Daisy walked through the downstairs, studying the colors and the values and the proportions of everything she was doing, trying to make sure it balanced, that it was interesting and new and different without being so far out that it humiliated Linc. The living room, dining room, and hall were done, but she wasn't happy with them.

"It's ordinary," she told Julia on the phone. "It's very pretty, but it's ordinary. Daisy Flattery wouldn't live here."

"That's because you're pleasing Linc. Get some paint, go in there, and please Daisy. What have you painted on canvas lately?"

"Nothing. I've just done walls and furniture."

"Well, there you are. Do some canvases for the walls. Better yet, do some canvases for you."

Daisy thought about it. She was tired of walls and patterns; it was time to get back to stories. "You're right. I'll lock the bedroom doors so all that these people will see upstairs is the bathroom. Everything else is done down here except for the kitchen. Maybe I'll go crazy in the kitchen. And I'll do some collages. There's a great secondhand place near the college that has a box full of lace and embroidery I could use to do a collage for the hall. And I'll paint. I've got a lot of stories I've thought of here that I want to paint. This is a wonderful place. You've got to come stay soon."

"I will," Julia said. "How's Linc?"

"Fine. He seems happy and his book is going well."

"I mean, how are Linc and you?"

Daisy thought about their morning jogs. "We're fine."

"After that kiss at the wedding, I thought you'd be more than fine."

Daisy tried to brush her off. "I think that was a fluke. He's not much interested. He likes little blondes, remember?"

"Yeah, but he married a bouncing brunette," Julia said dryly.

"He didn't have much choice."

Julia's snort was loud on the line. "Linc always has a choice. He's the most controlled guy I've ever met. If he married you, he wanted to."

Daisy felt a flare of hope. "Maybe."

"So how's Evan?" Julia's voice was carefully casual.

"Evan? Depressed, how else would Evan be?"

"Oh."

Daisy tried to remember something about Evan to share. "Come to think of it, he has seemed more depressed than usual. He mentioned you the other day. He said you had an interesting sense of humor."

"Oh."

Hello? Daisy raised her eyebrows at the phone. Evan and Julia? Well, stranger things had happened. She and Linc, for example.

"Come visit soon," she said to Julia.

"Go paint. I'll come when you've got a show ready for that gallery. Have you gone down there yet?"

"No, and it'll be a good long time yet before I do,"

Daisy said, but after she'd hung up she went upstairs happier than she'd been before. *I'll start to paint again,* she told herself, *as soon as I've picked up Jupiter.*

Jupiter was not a hit at first. He barked a lot, and developed a fondness for Linc that bordered on the pathological since Linc's first words on seeing him were "That's the most disgusting-looking animal I've ever seen."

Jupiter had only one eye, so he looked as if he were permanently winking. His tail was bent down at a right angle, he limped, and because he'd lost teeth on one side of his mouth, his tongue tended to hang out that side when he panted.

"I think he's darling." Daisy's heart bled for him every time she saw him. "Poor baby."

"Poor baby, my butt." Linc glared down at the little dog. "This is the luckiest dog in Prescott. You're a mess," he said to the dog. "We should put you out on the street with a cup to beg."

"*Linc.*"

"He could sell pencils. We'd make a fortune."

"Ignore him, baby." Daisy patted Jupiter's head, but Jupiter ignored her instead and attached himself to Linc. At first Linc would yell at her to come get the dog when it would sneak into his room, but on Friday, Daisy heard him talking to it when she went past his study door to go to her studio.

"You're worthless. Here. Have a biscuit."

A biscuit? He'd bought dog biscuits for Jupiter? The world was coming to an end.

She knocked on the door. "Do you want me to get Jupiter out of there?"

"No," Linc said from behind the door. "He just sneaks back in. This is a worthless dog."

"Yes, Linc," she said, and went away laughing silently.

On Saturday, Linc came downstairs to get the house ready for the party and finally noticed Daisy had redecorated.

"This looks great," he said as he wandered from room to room. "I mean, it really does. Did you do all this? It's sort of colorful, but great." He stopped in front of the painting on the mantel. It was painted in Daisy's primitive style of tiny vivid brushstrokes, and it showed a Victorian house sitting in what looked like a lush green jungle populated by a lot of unblinking leaf-green eyes. A girl in a bright peach dress stood in the foreground, looking pensive.

"There's a lot of detail here." Linc leaned in for a closer look. "You can see in the windows of the house and—" His voice broke off.

"Do you like it? This is one of my favorites."

"There's a headless body on the couch in the downstairs room." Linc turned to look at her. "You painted a headless body on a couch?"

Daisy nodded. "It's Lizzie Borden's house. It really is. I found a photograph. They had a picture of the body too. It's not really headless. Almost, but not quite."

Be open-minded, Linc told himself. It was the least he owed her, but he was still thrown. Headless bodies? "Lizzie Borden."

"That's her father on the couch. Her stepmother's in the upstairs bedroom. If you look really hard, you can see her feet at the edge of the windowsill."

Linc nodded, coping. "Her feet."

"You do know the story? 'Lizzie Borden took an ax and'—"

"I know the story." Linc's resolve broke. "Whatever possessed you to paint it?"

"Probably my father and stepmother," Daisy said grimly.

Linc changed the subject. "Why is she looking so calm?"

"Well, nobody knows for sure if she did it. So she's either standing there innocently while someone evil frames her for the crime, or she's planning her defense. You choose."

They stood together and looked at the painting for a while, and Linc realized that even though he was still thrown, he liked the painting. There was something about it that was so Daisy, bright and colorful and passionate with strange things hidden inside. Amazing. "Does every one of your paintings have a story?" he asked.

"Oh, yes," Daisy said blithely. "The one in the dining room is based on the legend of Etain."

"What happened to Etain?" he asked, knowing it was going to be horrible.

"A jealous witch turned her into a butterfly, and she got blown into a wineglass and a beautiful queen drank her."

Linc nodded, trying to be supportive. "Drank her."

"Yes. And then nine months later the queen gave birth to a baby girl, and Etain's lover waited for her to grow up again so he could marry her. Then they lived happily ever after. Something horrible happened to the witch, but I can't remember what. Her name was Fuamach; you'd think that would be enough of a punishment."

"Are all your paintings about horrible things?"

Daisy pulled away, surprised. "These aren't horrible. These have happy endings. Lizzie was never convicted, and Etain lived happily ever after forever with Mider. I can't do the really unhappy ones. I tried to paint Deirdre once, but I ended up burning the canvas."

The memory of it clouded her face, and Linc found himself wanting to know all about her paintings because it was telling him so much about her. "What happened to Deirdre?"

"A man she didn't like forced her to marry him, and she killed herself."

Linc looked down at her, startled, but she was gazing serenely at Lizzie, apparently without ulterior motive. "The peach dress is nice, isn't it? It looks like Victorian passion."

He looked back at the painting. "Was Lizzie passionate?"

"You'd have to be pretty passionate to hack up your father and stepmother, wouldn't you?"

"I thought she wasn't convicted."

"She wasn't, but I still think she did it." Daisy gave her alter ego one last look and then turned to survey the living room. "I covered up the holes and the cracks in the furniture. You really can't tell, can you?"

"It looks great," he said sincerely, and then shot one last nervous glance over his shoulder at Lizzie.

Daisy was moving on, like a blur of brightness through the pastel room. "I'm buying flowers this afternoon. And I'm making stew in case anyone wants to eat when they get here."

Linc tensed. Stew. That was bad; these people didn't eat stew, they ate coq au vin. "They won't want to eat. Forget the stew and we'll just have drinks."

Daisy looked apologetic, and he kicked himself for being so blatant, but all she said was "We'd better set up a bar on the buffet, then."

"Make a note to pick up liquor," he told her, and went into the dining room to see how much space there was on the buffet. Over it was a primitive still life of a table covered with blue and white checks. The table held a vase of flowers, a bowl of fruit, and a glass of pink wine. He leaned closer. There was definitely a butterfly in the wine.

He sighed, and then he started to laugh. Lizzie Borden in the living room and a drowned butterfly in the dining room. The place looked like *Better Homes & Gardens,* but it was really Charles Addams. He looked over at the flower garlands that graced the hall, wondering what details they hid. "This is really great," he told her when she'd followed him. He patted her shoulder. "Cute. You did a good job. Uh, did you hide anything in the flowers and stuff on the walls?"

"No." Daisy stopped, clearly intrigued. "That's a good idea. This place is too boring. I could . . ."

"No, no." Linc waved his hand at her. "It's great just as it is. Really." He looked around again and was surprised to realize he was telling the truth. "It really is. Nice going, Daize."

Linc's praise meant more to Daisy than she wanted to admit. It wasn't easy being Daisy Blaise. She slaved over the party, making lists of things that had to be done and leaving reminders for herself all over the house on multicolored sticky notes, and then made sure that every line on every list was crossed off and every note was followed, finished, and thrown away before anyone arrived. It wasn't her style, and it made her crazy and tense and tired, but she was Linc's wife, throwing Linc's party, and she was terrified she'd screw it up, so she watched him for clues. She'd almost served stew until she'd seen Linc's face when she mentioned it. They'd need cloth napkins and wine sauce, and it wasn't much consolation that she always threw some wine in her stew. She didn't think that uncorking the bottle and slopping some in counted as wine sauce, so she left the Crock-Pot on low in case she and Linc were hungry after everyone left and concentrated on getting the house as clean and polished as possible.

An hour before they left for the faculty club, she sat on her bed in her white dress and shook from the tension. It was going to be awful. She'd be on display, just as she used to be with her father. Chickie would be nice no matter what, and Booker and Lacey and Evan would be too, but they'd know she wasn't right, wasn't their kind of people, and that would be terrible for Linc. And Crawford was such a snob, he'd say something. And Caroline...

I should never have done this, she thought. *I can't be like these people. I'll never fit in and I'll embarrass Linc and—*

"Daisy?" Linc called, and she took deep breaths, the way he'd taught her, and went out to join him.

She stayed quiet and polite all evening, terrified she'd do the wrong thing, and Chickie and Lacey both asked her if she was all right. "Just fine," she said brightly, and Evan said, "You probably have something catching," and wandered off to the buffet more from momentum than fear of disease. By the end of the evening Daisy had relaxed a little, but she clutched again when they got back from the club, and they all came into the house.

Evan came to her rescue in the living room without really meaning to. "This painting is really excellent." Evan peered closely at Lizzie's house. "Of course, the artist will never receive the recognition he's due since it's a primitive, but it's excellent. Who did it?"

"I did," Daisy said.

Evan's eyebrows rose above his glasses. "Did you do the collages in the hall too?"

"Yes." Daisy relaxed again, but she kept an eye on Caroline while she talked. Linc might be determined to say no, but Caroline looked pretty determined too, drawing Linc down onto the flowered couch with her. Speaking of determined . . . she turned back to Evan. "Julia gave me the idea for the collages."

"Then you should invite her to see them," Evan said with uncharacteristic firmness. "Invite her soon."

"All right." Julia and Evan. Daisy shook her head.

Evan seemed a little taken aback by his own audacity and changed the subject. "Do you sell your work?"

"I try, but not since I've come to Prescott."

"It's quite good. You should take it to the gallery and show it to Bill. I'd like to see your other things sometime, if I may." Then, as if he realized he was sounding optimistic, he added, "Although you probably won't want to show them to me."

"Of course I want to show them to you." Daisy put her arm around him. There was something about Evan that made you want to comfort him, something beyond his rampant gloom. "Are you hungry?" she asked without thinking. "I made stew."

"Yes." Evan turned toward the kitchen bravely. "It will probably give me heartburn, but I am hungry, and I would like some stew."

The Bookers followed them into the kitchen.

"Daisy, this house is darling," Lacey said.

"Something smells really good in here," her husband said pointedly.

"I made stew," Daisy said, and forgot about Linc and gourmet cooking. "Would you like some?"

Crawford had trailed along after them. "Nothing like a little woman who can cook," he said, and when Chickie stuck her head in the door to see what they were doing, she agreed.

"You're just going to have to give me that recipe, honey."

"Better taste it first." Daisy handed Chickie a stack of bowls, Lacey the silverware, and Booker the paper napkins. "We're not formal here," she told them. She handed Evan the Crock-Pot and shooed them all into the dining room.

She went back for a pitcher of milk and a basket of

bread and came out in time to hear Booker say, "There are whole mushrooms in here." He speared one with his fork. "Real, whole mushrooms."

Linc and Caroline joined them, and Daisy watched with her fingers crossed as they sat crowded around the big oak table and talked about the paintings and the house and the food.

Caroline sat next to Linc. "This is really wonderful." She looked over at Daisy, her head almost touching Linc's shoulder. "It must be terrific to be a housewife and do all these little decorating and cooking things. My apartment is just wall-to-wall books and a microwave."

"Thank you," Daisy said. *Drop dead, Caroline.*

"Daisy's a painter," Linc said. "She's not a housewife; she's an artist."

"There's nothing wrong with being a housewife," Daisy said over her bowl. "It's an art too. I just don't have the concentration to sustain it. Linc gets food when I remember to cook it and feeds himself when I don't."

"I like it that way." Linc smiled at her.

She smiled back at him. *Put that in your pipe, Caroline. And then get out of my house.*

Jupiter came down to see everyone as they were leaving.

"My God, what is that?" Caroline shrieked.

"That's Jupiter." Daisy glared at her. "My dog."

Caroline smirked and looked over at Linc to exchange mutual glances of contempt, but he wasn't playing.

"Jupiter's an original." Linc looked down at the dog with pride. "He's not one of those soulless purebreds."

Jupiter lurched on his bad hip and fell over sideways.

"No, that he isn't," Booker agreed. "What is he anyway?"

"Part beagle," Daisy said. "And part a few other things."

"He looks like he's been recycled," Evan said. "A very practical dog."

"A dog with personality." Lacey Booker bent down to pet him. Jupiter rolled over on his back in ecstasy.

"What a sweet baby," Chickie said.

"We've got to be going." Crawford hugged Daisy, letting his hand slide down to her rear end.

After their good-byes, Daisy closed the door behind them with a sigh. "If we could lose Crawford and Caroline, we'd have a very nice group of people there."

Linc loosened his tie and started up the stairs. "Well, we can't."

Daisy folded her arms and called after him. "She keeps undressing you with her eyes, and he keeps groping my rear."

Linc turned back. "In that case, I'm a lot more worried about him. I'll say something to him tomorrow."

"No." Daisy let her arms drop. "Forget it. I was just kidding. How was it, do you think? Was it all right, the stew and all?"

"It was great." Linc started back up the stairs. "You really pulled it off. Good going, Daize."

"Thanks," she said a little sadly to his retreating back. She wasn't sure what she wanted to hear from him, but somehow, what he'd said wasn't enough. Maybe a pat on the back. Maybe a big hug. Maybe...

Forget it, she told herself. *He's cold, cold, cold.*

She washed the dishes and checked to make sure she'd finished her list of things to do for the day before she went up to bed. She felt very organized and very adult and very alone, and she missed Daisy Flattery more than she could say.

Daisy's life after the party fell into an easy rhythm, and she began to lose her Daisy Flattery regrets.

At six they'd jog, Daisy eventually building up enough stamina to keep running for the whole hour. Then they'd have breakfast, and Linc would work on his book, and Daisy would go back to bed, crawling into the rumpled sheets with a pleasure that was almost sexual. Linc left for the college every day at nine, and Daisy got up again every day at noon and worked on the house, painting secret things in the garlands on the walls and furniture that first appalled and then amused Linc. They had dinner together at six, talking about her paintings of driven women and his book of rebellious women. It was Daisy's favorite part of the day, and she thought it might be Linc's too, because he was never late and he never tried to hurry her through the meal or took his food upstairs on a tray. She was learning so much from him, not just about his book but about her own work. He brought her home pictures of Rosa Parks so she could finish the painting, and he talked with her about the ideas she wanted to use, what they meant to him, which helped her figure out what they meant to her. They talked about his book too, about birth control and what it meant to women, and he asked her questions and listened to her answers, even once saying, "Wait a minute, I want to write that down," and leaving the table for pencil and paper while she went dizzy with pride and pleasure. She'd never known conversation could be so intense and so satisfying and so ultimately frustrating, because making conversation with him told her what making love with him would be like, just as intimate and intense.

After dinner Linc worked on his book until eleven, and Daisy took her frustration upstairs and painted until three or four in the morning, first Rosa Parks and then, inspired by Linc, Margaret Sanger. The Sanger painting was different somehow, angrier in the reds and blacks she found herself using and the sharp forms with which she surrounded the intense central figure draped in gray, her tiny black eyes like tiny black holes in the canvas.

"That's amazing," Linc said when she showed it to him in November. "That's my book. If I sell this book, maybe we could use it for the cover design. Would you mind?"

And Daisy had shook her head no because she was too dazzled to talk.

"I like your other stuff too," he told her before he went back to his room to write, "but this is something different. You're really growing here."

I am, Daisy thought. Not enough yet, she still wasn't where she should be, but the Sanger painting was stronger than her earlier work. The deal was working.

Except I want it all, she told herself. *I love the intellectual stuff we have, but I want the physical stuff too.*

Maybe one night when they were talking, arguing passionately about some idea, she could just lean over and kiss him. She tried to tell herself the story, how Linc would sweep her into his arms and say, "My God, how could I have been so blind?" but it wouldn't come out true somehow. That wasn't Linc. He'd be embarrassed and pull back and he'd take his meals on a tray and she'd lose the wonderful conversations she counted on. It was the first time she couldn't make a story come out right, and it rattled her a little.

You have more right now than most women have ever dreamed of, she told herself. *Don't get greedy.*

Linc wasn't sure when he first realized he'd lost his grip on his story. The realization came gradually, built up in short encounters like the day he answered the front door to find a little old lady dressed in three different brightly colored cardigans and a lime green skirt. She handed him a pie and said, "This is for Daisy. You must be Linc. You have a lovely wife." She peered up at him. "Reminds me of myself when I was young."

She dresses like you too, Linc thought, but all he said was "Thank you, Mrs.—uh . . ."

"Armbruster. You tell Daisy I said thank you."

"I certainly will."

He took the pie into the kitchen and put it on the counter in front of Daisy. "Who's Mrs. Armbruster?"

"Our next door neighbor on the right. She's very nice. I helped her with her lawn mower yesterday. She said she was going to make us a rhubarb pie."

This is not what I had in mind, Linc thought, but he didn't say anything and Daisy went on. "Mr. Antonelli lives on our other side. He used to teach romance languages at the college before he retired. He said we needed to put potassium on our dogwood or it won't bloom. And Dr. Banks lives across the street. He helped me catch Annie when she got out the other day. Next to him is . . ."

"Daisy?" Linc gritted his teeth to keep from saying something tactless like *Please don't let people know how weird you are,* but Daisy read his mind anyway and flushed.

"I know. I'm supposed to lie low. But these are our neighbors. We have to be neighborly."

He thought about saying, *no, we don't,* but telling Daisy not to be neighborly was like telling Jupiter not to get fleas. They both meant well, but they just naturally attracted other living beings to them.

Then Evan came to him at school and asked if it was all right that he was dropping by the yellow house three or four times a week in the afternoon. He assured Linc his attentions were honorable, and Linc nodded, bemused by the thought of Evan seducing Daisy. Crawford mentioned that Chickie sure enjoyed having lunch with Daisy every day, and shortly after that Booker told him that Lacey was coming over in the afternoons to help Daisy paint ivy leaves in the bathroom so she could learn to do them in her dining room. "Do I want ivy in my dining room?" Booker asked him, and Linc said, "If Lacey wants it there, do you have a choice?"

He'd also lost his grip on keeping his professional and personal lives separate. Daisy argued with him about bringing his tutorial students home to work in the dining room like the other professors did, and he finally gave in just to end the argument. After that, students regularly stopped by and used the dining room as a study table, checking out the cookie jar to see if Daisy had felt like baking, baking themselves if she hadn't. Linc worried that they'd bother her, cut into her painting time, but she told him that she liked them, and that they were very respectful of her work.

Olivia, one of the students, told Linc, "You think they're just pretty pictures, but they have whole lives in them, wonderful lives of weird women who do something strong and important and dangerous. And they're always true." She'd stopped for a moment and then said, "You've probably already noticed this, but they're all like Daisy."

"I hadn't noticed," Linc had said a little stiffly. There was something so intimate about Daisy's painting that discussing it with a student seemed wrong, invasive, *personal,* and Olivia had looked at him sadly before she went back to the study table.

Even though he was aware of what was going on, Linc didn't realize the extent to which his house and his wife had become part of the fabric of Prescott, until a phone call sent him home unexpectedly one Tuesday in late November.

He met Chickie coming out the door.

"Hello, darling." She hugged him and then stepped aside so he could get through the front door. "Daisy's with Lacey upstairs painting the bathroom."

Linc knew there was something different about Chickie, but he couldn't put his finger on it. He watched her walk out to the sidewalk and realized she wasn't swaying. She wasn't drunk. It was the first time he'd seen her completely sober.

He shook his head and went inside.

Two of his students, Olivia and Larry, were working over their notes on World War II at the dining room table while Liz sprawled across Olivia's lap and Annie batted at Larry's pen. He started to tell Annie to get off the table, but Andrew, another student, came out of the kitchen with a bowl.

"Decide now. Nuts in the chocolate chips or not?"

"Nuts," said a voice from the living room, and he turned to see Tracy, yet another student, lying on the couch with Jupiter on his back on top of her. She was scratching his stomach slowly, and Jupiter looked as if he were in ecstasy.

"You'll probably break a tooth." Evan came out of the kitchen behind Andrew, holding an apple. "Shell pieces. There's always a risk."

There were too many people in his house. Linc looked around a little frantically. "Is Daisy here?"

"Upstairs with Lacey in the bathroom." Olivia waved her hand toward the stairs. "They're finishing the ivy today. It looks super."

"She's going to do the kitchen in trompe l'oeil." Tracy sat up. "She said she'd teach me."

"Have you seen her last painting?" Evan asked him. "It's Sanger. Daisy's really got something. Of course, it will never be recognized. I tried to get her a gallery show, but Bill's booked through next year." He bit into the apple. "Probably covered with chemicals." He wandered out the front door.

Linc watched him go before he turned back to Tracy. "There are a lot of people here. Is it always like this?"

"Pretty much." Tracy lay back down, much to Jupiter's delight. "That's why we call it the Hive."

"The Hive?"

"Little yellow house, always busy. The Hive."

"Nothing about Killer Bees?" Linc asked suspiciously.

"No." Larry looked up from his notes. "Are there any?"

"No." Linc went upstairs to find Daisy.

"You're much better at this than I am," Daisy was saying to Lacey when he reached the bathroom.

"I like this." Lacey gazed at the wall with satisfaction. "Teach me to paint something else."

"Like what?" Daisy put her brush to soak. "We're almost finished in here."

"Roses, daffodils, tulips, irises..."

"Not in here," Linc said from the doorway. "Have a heart. I brush my teeth in here. I have hangovers in here."

"Well, hi." Daisy smiled up at him, and for some reason he forgot to breathe. It wasn't stress this time; he never felt stressed when he looked at Daisy now.

She stood up and walked toward him and he held

out his hand to her. She took it and stood close and said, "What brings you home?"

Then he remembered and his stress levels rose again. "My mother called."

"Oh, dear," Daisy said.

"Don't mind me," Lacey said. "You go talk. I'll stay here and finish the painting."

EIGHT

THEY WENT INTO Daisy's bedroom and sat on the bed, and Linc thought for a moment about how great it would be if they were alone and he could just have his arms around her. It would be such a comfort, such a distraction from all his problems.

"There are a lot of people here," Linc said. "How can you stand this?"

Daisy blinked at him, surprised. "Stand what? They let me alone. If I go in the studio, nobody bothers me. They answer the phone and take messages and since they've been here, Crawford doesn't stop by in the afternoons."

Linc's grip on her hand tightened. "What?"

"He used to come by and ring the doorbell, and I'd just stay inside and wait until he went away. When the kids started coming over, he gave up."

He scowled down at her. "Why didn't you tell me?"

Daisy shrugged. "What could you have done?"

"What I should have done the first day: told him I'd break his fingers if he ever touched you."

Daisy laughed, a soft little chuckle. "Did you ever actually break anyone's fingers?"

Linc's annoyance faded with her chuckle. "No, but as your brother from New Jersey, I figure Crawford's the place to start."

"You're not my brother."

His eyes met hers and he felt a flash of heat that rocked his complacency.

Daisy swallowed and said, "What did your mother want?"

"Oh, Lord." He put his head in his hand. "I forgot. She's coming to stay. She'll be at Wil's for Christmas, so she's coming to stay with us for the first week in December. That's next week."

"Oh." Daisy smiled brightly. "That will be nice. Get a room at the inn."

Linc patted her hand, knowing she was going to hate the next part. "There are none. I tried. It's Winterfest on campus. And I think she wants to stay here anyway. She knows we have a spare bedroom."

"No, we don't," Daisy said, puzzled.

"My mother, like everyone else we know, thinks we sleep together."

"Oh."

"It's just for a week," Linc said lamely, knowing that a week with his mother would be hell.

Daisy nodded, her head a little wobbly on her neck. "We'll be fine. Really. We will. She can have this bed, and I'll sleep in your room. No big deal. And she'll get along great with Evan; he never smiles either. By the way, Evan is coming here for Christmas Eve."

Linc's visions of Christmas as just another great dinner with Daisy disappeared. "Why?"

"Because he's not going home, and because Julia will be here." Daisy grinned. "Which is why he's not going home. And I asked Art too, and Evan introduced me to Bill from the gallery and he's nice and alone, and things were getting so big that I asked the Crawfords and the Bookers too. It will be cozy. Pansy will be in the Bahamas, but maybe your mother will stay."

Oh, yes, his mother introduced into that group was all they'd need to make the holidays perfect. "Maybe she won't."

He sounded so gloomy that Daisy peered up at him, trying to read the expression on his face. "Are you unhappy about this?"

"No." Linc straightened up. "It's just not what I had planned."

"I know." Daisy recognized that he wasn't talking about his mother. "I was supposed to lay low and stay away from people. But that's hard for me."

"I know." He put his arm around her and pulled her close in a semi-hug, and it felt so good, she closed her eyes. "It was a dumb plan," he went on. "We've been married for almost three months. Is there anyone in town who doesn't know you by your first name?"

Daisy nodded again, eager to reassure him. "Lots. I spend most of my time here, painting. I've gotten so much done, Linc. Really good work, because I haven't worried about money or anything. This is all because of you." She kissed him on the cheek. "This is great."

He froze for a moment and then tightened his arm around her. "My book's done."

"What? You're kidding!"

"Nope." He grinned like a little kid. "I have to edit it and smooth things out a little, but essentially, it's done. And that's not all. I've got a publisher."

Daisy shrieked and hugged him, and he laughed.

"A publisher." Daisy glowed at him. "Imagine. Just like that."

"Just like that, hell." Linc tried to frown at her but she could see the delight still bubbling underneath. "I submitted the damn thing eight places in the past year before I got anyone to look at it."

Daisy was incredulous. Linc was one of the most brilliant people she'd ever known, not to mention a great writer with a great subject. "Eight places turned *you* down?"

Linc laughed and pulled her to him again. "You know, you're good for my ego, kid. Stick around."

She was distracted by the hug, but the enormity of what he'd said came back. "But wasn't it awful? Eight times?"

"Well, it wasn't fun. But that's the way it goes."

He'd kept going after eight rejections. She'd given up after one, after Bill, who'd become a friend, told her that he already had his shows booked. She hadn't even checked with other galleries in other cities. "You know, I'm learning a lot from you," she told him.

"This has worked out great for both of us." Linc rubbed his thumb along her cheek affectionately. "This is one terrific deal."

I can think of some things that would make it more terrific, she thought, but all she said was "And we've got six months left to go before the deal's over. Think of all the things we can get done. You can write another book."

He'd dropped his arm from her shoulders. "Let me get this one done first." He stood up. "Mother will be driving down next week. Do you need me to do anything?"

"No." Daisy felt cold as he moved away. It had been nice with his arm around her. "Just be home for dinner and the evenings; I'll fake the days. Maybe she naps."

"I doubt it. I don't think she sleeps."

Linc's mother drove in the next week, and Daisy went out to the car to help her with her bag. "How was your drive?" She moved to take Gertrude's suitcase. "You must be exhausted."

Gertrude gave up her suitcase without a fight. "Yes."

Daisy looked at her closely. She was even paler than usual. "Hot tea." Daisy put her arm around Gertrude and led her into the house. "And a nap. We'll have dinner at home tonight, just the three of us. You can relax."

Gertrude nodded and followed Daisy up the stairs

to Daisy's bedroom. Daisy turned back the counter-
pane and left her to go make tea.

When Daisy came back, Gertrude was in bed
looking shockingly frail. Gertrude had been such an
overwhelming presence that she'd seemed massive.
Now she looked translucent and brittle, like very old,
very thin china.

"Let me put some pillows behind you." Daisy sup-
ported her firmly with her arm while she stacked the
pillows behind the older woman. "I've brought you
tea and some cookies that one of Linc's students
baked."

"Thank you." Gertrude's voice was faint, and
Daisy was really alarmed. She ran downstairs and
called the doctor who lived across the street.

"This is Daisy Blaise. It's my mother-in-law. She's
really ill and I don't think she can make it across the
street. It's either you or the rescue squad."

"I'll come," Dr. Banks said. "The rescue squad
makes too much noise."

Half an hour later he came downstairs. "Flu."

Daisy felt her own stomach heave at the thought.
"Flu?"

"She'll be sick for about a week. This is that nasty
strain they've got up north. And we want to keep it
up north. This place is in quarantine."

Quarantine. With Gertrude. And Linc. Oh, Lord. "Can Linc go to work?"

"Only if he promises not to breathe on the students. You keep the students out, understand?"

Daisy nodded. The last thing she needed was a lot of people while she coped with Gertrude, a woman she was fairly certain saw illness as something only weaker people encountered. "I understand. What about Gertrude? What do I do?"

"Keep her warm and give her plenty of liquids. She should be through this by Friday."

"Great." Daisy sighed. "Thank you. I know you don't make house calls, so I really appreciate this."

"Across the street isn't a house call." He looked around at Daisy's painted walls. "Besides, it's a nice house."

I'm going to miss living here, she thought as she watched him cross the street. Such nice people. Such a nice town. Such a nice house.

She lettered a sign that said Flu Quarantine and taped it to the front door and then went to make vegetable soup. Vegetable soup had a lot of liquid in it.

"Is that a joke?" Linc gestured to the sign as he came through the front door, and Daisy flapped her hand at him to shush him.

"Shhh. Your mother's upstairs, and she's really sick. You can go up and sit with her after dinner."

"Do I have to?" Linc asked appalled.

"Yes." Daisy restrained herself from saying something exasperated. "You have to."

After dinner that night, Linc reluctantly climbed the stairs.

"Read her this." Daisy shoved a book into his hands as he went up, and he carried it with him when he went in to see his mother.

He was as shocked as Daisy had been at the change in her. She looked old and fragile, not the Iron Mother he'd grown up with. "Hello," he said softly. "Daisy sent me up to read to you. Would you like that or would you rather just sleep?"

"I would like a little reading." She tried to focus on him. "I have been sleeping all day. And the dinner was very good. Real homemade soup." She sighed a little. "Daisy is a good woman."

"Yes, she is." It was unlike his mother to be so mellow, and it made Linc nervous. "Let's see what she's given us to read." Linc opened the book and then laughed.

"What is it?"

" 'There was a man in the land of Uz, whose name was Job; and that man was blameless and upright,' " Linc began. He looked over at his mother, who was blameless and upright, and she smiled weakly and he smiled back, and for one moment he felt united with her in affection for Daisy.

"This is good." His mother relaxed into her pillow. "I feel better. The boils I have not got yet."

" 'He feared God and turned away from evil,' " Linc read on, and his mother closed her eyes, and when he glanced over as he read, she was smiling slightly, and she looked comforted. *God bless Daisy*, he thought, and read on.

Later that evening, after Daisy had checked on Gertrude and given her aspirin for her fever, she went into Linc's bedroom and climbed into bed with him. He was still reading the Bible.

"Job." He shook his head. "I would never have thought of it, but she liked it." He looked over at her, smiling. "She really liked it."

"I love it."

He watched as Daisy wriggled down in the bed to get comfortable. His mattress was harder than hers, and it took her a while to get situated, and he couldn't take his eyes off her as she punched pillows and tried to find a softer place for her hip. Finally she was where she wanted to be, and she went on.

"Job's wonderful, although not the arguing bits. The good stuff's the part where God rips a strip off

Job for whining. Here." She took the book from him and flipped forward a few pages. "Chapter Thirty-eight. 'Where were you when I laid the foundation of the earth? Tell me if you have understanding. Who determined its measurements—surely you know!' I love that bit, God getting sarcastic. 'Or who stretched the line upon it? On what were its bases sunk, or who laid its cornerstone, when the morning stars sang together, and all the sons of God shouted for joy.' "

Daisy put the book down on her lap and stared into space, a delighted smile on her face. "Except I see the daughters of God shouting too. All the people together, shouting for joy, and the morning stars singing." She closed the book and leaned back on her pillows. "Our church was gray stone on the inside and it was so beautiful. The sun would come through the stained glass windows and warm the wooden pews, and our minister would read this stuff and I'd feel so safe." She turned and looked into his eyes. "I never felt that safe again until I moved in with you. Thank you."

Linc was speechless. The combined effects of his mother, frail and ill and needing him, and Daisy, warm and healthy and trusting him, left him dizzy. *Stay with me,* he wanted to say. *Be my wife.* Then the room started to spin around and he realized he wasn't breathing. He drew in a deep breath and took the book from her. "I like keeping you safe. What's your favorite book?"

"Ecclesiastes. Song of Songs. Esther. Ruth." She snuggled down into her pillow. "Different things for different moods." She yawned. "If you hear me get up later, I'm just checking on your mom. Don't worry."

She closed her eyes, and he looked down at her pale face framed by the splash of dark curls on her pillow. She was so sweet and warm, and he loved her so much.

The thought startled him. *I love her like a sister,* he told himself. *Except that I want her too.* Evil thoughts for a man with a Bible on his lap.

He flipped through the pages until he chanced into the middle of Song of Songs and read, "I come to my garden, my sister, my bride," and thought, *everything really is in the Bible.* Then he went back to the beginning and read, "Oh that you would kiss me with the kisses of your mouth! For your love is better than wine."

That's it, he thought, and put the book on his bedside table. Enough Bible. Then he turned out the light and fell asleep, thinking about Daisy, only inches away from him.

• • •

The next night his mother was worse, and he read only a little more of Job before he closed the book and said, "You're tired. I'll read more tomorrow."

"You have your father's voice." Gertrude rolled her head on her pillow so she could see him in the lamplight. "I close my eyes and I can see him when you read. You look so much like him."

Linc sat frozen. His mother had never talked like this before. *It's the fever,* he told himself.

"I loved him so much." Her voice was weak, barely a thread. "It was God's miracle that he loved me. So big and strong, just like you. And then I lost him." A tear rolled down her cheek. "I tell myself it is part of God's plan, but I have been so lonely. Eighteen years."

Eighteen years alone. Linc shuddered at the coldness of it.

"I did not love you enough." Gertrude's tears were coming faster. "Later, I was better. I was better with Wil and Ken. But I did not love you enough then. I am sorry."

"*No.*" His embarrassment was agony, but much worse was how helpless he was to stop her pain. "No, it's all right. You were a good mother."

She shook her head weakly on the pillow. "No. But now it is all right. You have Daisy. Now you will get all the love I could not give you." She was openly crying now, the tears rolling down her cheeks, and Linc felt the room begin to swoop. This couldn't be happening. He had to stop it.

"Listen." He grabbed her hand and held on tightly. "You took care of me. I had plenty to eat, and my clothes were always clean, and you never interfered or pushed me or made me feel like I wasn't a good son. You gave me space to grow up and you took care of me. And I was fine. Really."

"You deserved more," Gertrude insisted, her eyes bright with tears.

He ran his hand through his hair, unsure of what to say next. "I'm just glad you didn't die." He stopped when he realized that was true. And he didn't want her alone and cold either. "Listen, I don't like this stuff about you being lonely. Why don't you move down here? We'll take care of you."

She cried even harder, and he couldn't understand why, and he sat frozen until Daisy walked in and took the Bible out of his hands.

"Go away," she said. "Crying is women's stuff." When he didn't move she looked at him more closely and said, "Breathe, Blaise," and he sucked in a deep breath. "Now go away."

He stood up and she took his place on the bed. She

pulled out a tissue and gently blotted Gertrude's tears away. "I know he's awful," she teased, "but you shouldn't cry like this. You need all the liquid you've got; the doctor said so."

Gertrude kept crying silently, the tears sliding down her cheeks faster now, and Linc felt like hell.

"What did you say?" Daisy asked Linc, but she wasn't accusing him, thank God. "What were you talking about?"

"My dad." Linc took another deliberate breath. "And I told her I thought she should move down here so we could take care of her."

He watched Daisy's eyebrows go up in surprise, and then she said, "Of course. That's a good idea. Go away now. Make some tea."

He didn't understand, but he went downstairs and made tea for all of them and found cookies that Daisy had made that day, and when he went back upstairs half an hour later, he met her coming out of her room.

"She's sleeping." She put her hand on his cheek. "You poor baby. Are you all right?"

Linc slumped against the wall. "She's *never* said things like that before."

She let her hand fall from his cheek to his shoulder, and he missed the comfort of her palm on his face. "She's sick," Daisy told him. "It makes people feel vulnerable. They say things they keep hidden when they're feeling strong. Let's have the tea downstairs."

She took the tray from him and led him back downstairs, and he watched her and remembered his mother's loneliness, and thought, *What am I going to do when she leaves?* The thought was so bleak that he even drank tea with her although he hated the stuff.

Linc's mother got steadily stronger and never referred to that evening again. But they finished Job, and Linc felt as though a knotted place inside had been freed. It shouldn't matter now, after all these years, that his mother loved him, had loved him then, and was sorry that she hadn't loved him more, but it did. For the first time he saw her as a real person with regrets instead of just a demanding shadow in his life, and when he let himself care about her, the world around him became an easier place.

The last thing she said to him before she left at the end of the week was "Take care of Daisy. She is so good for you."

"I will." He kissed her good-bye gently. "Take care of yourself. If you feel sick again, we'll come up and get you. Are you sure you don't want to move down here?"

"I am sure." She put her hand on his cheek as she must have seen Daisy do half a dozen times that week. Another surprise. "You must take care of yourself too. You are very pale."

"I'm always pale." He kissed her cheek. "Be careful on the drive home."

Daisy heaved a sigh of relief when Gertrude was gone. She liked her, but sleeping with Linc for a week had been too difficult. It wasn't just that he had a nice, large, hard body, the kind of body a woman could hold on to during great, cataclysmic sex. She'd never actually had great, cataclysmic sex, but she was sure that was what she'd have with Linc. No, it wasn't just his body, it was more that he was Linc, stubborn, brilliant, kind, rude, fascinating Linc, who scratched Jupiter's tummy while he watched the game on TV and crooned dumb dog songs to him during the commercials. She'd heard him once singing, "Daisy Blaise had a real dumb dog, and Jupiter was his name/Oh, Ju-Ju-Ju-pi-ter/Ju-Ju-Ju-pi-ter/Ju-Ju-Ju-pi-ter/And Jupiter was his name, oh." When she'd looked in, Jupiter was on his back in Linc's lap, waving his legs languidly in all directions while Linc scratched his stomach. They both looked ridiculous and she loved them both so much, she felt tears start in her eyes.

There were so many layers to Linc, and they were all inside that great body. She definitely had to get out of his bed. And she wasn't sleeping well. Between her concern for Gertrude and her lust for Linc, it had been a rough week. Well, at least it was all over and they could get back to normal living. She went into the dining room and found Linc sitting at the table.

"What are you doing? Are you hungry?" she asked, and he turned his pale face to her, and she saw his eyes were dulled. She felt his forehead. It was burning.

Terrific. "You have the flu. Get into bed. I'll call Evan. He can proctor your finals."

"I'm all right," he said, and she said, "No, this is contagious. You stay home. Go upstairs."

Daisy couldn't decide whether Linc was sicker than Gertrude, or if it was just that he hated being sick so much that he seemed sicker. She brought him books and tea and soup and the radio and the TV, and he still thrashed around feverishly unless she was in the room with him. She read to him from his history books, and her voice seemed to calm him, the words keeping his mind off his aches until he got so sick, he didn't care anymore.

His fever went up, and one night she woke up and found him standing dazed in the hallway.

"What are you doing?" she scolded him. "Back into bed."

"I thought it was midnight."

"It's three-thirty, and even if it was midnight, you're still not supposed to be wandering around."

"I thought you'd gone," he said, and she realized he'd thought it was Cinderella's midnight.

"No. I won't leave you. Get back into bed."

She tucked him back in and he said, "Come in here with me. I'm cold," and she slipped into bed beside him and held him next to her warmth until he was quiet again.

In the morning his fever had broken, and hers began.

Linc still felt like hell the next day, but he knew just by looking at Daisy that she was worse.

"I can get up." She pulled weakly at his arm. "You're still sick."

"I'm not that sick." Linc put his hand on her cheek. "I'm all right. Get back in bed."

"No." She had crawled out of bed and staggered past him out onto the landing. When she turned to go down the stairs, she put out her hand for the rail and missed, and as she fell forward, Linc caught her and picked her up, his heart pounding from the adrenaline rush he'd gotten when she'd started to topple. He carried her into her room and pulled back the covers and made her crawl into bed, and then he popped the thermometer into her mouth.

"Stay there." He tucked in the covers tightly around her. "I'll put water on for tea."

He could tell Daisy wanted to argue, but she was too sick. Linc sympathized; he'd never felt as bad in his life as he had the past week. No wonder his mother had cried. He brought a tray of tea and crackers up and put it on the table. Then he checked her temperature. "One hundred and one." He shook the thermometer down and put it in his own mouth and crawled in bed beside her.

"That's got my germs on it," Daisy said, and he looked at her with disdain over the thermometer. "Oh, right. We've got the same thing."

A minute later he took the thermometer out and looked at it. "Just under one hundred. That's lower than yesterday, right?"

"Right." She closed her eyes. "You were one-oh-two yesterday."

"Good. I'm the one getting better, so I'm the boss."

"Ha."

"Shut up. We're going to be smart about this. We're going to sleep and drink juice and tea until we float, and we are not going to go charging around like we're healthy when we know we're not."

"Does we mean you too?"

"Of course it means me too. What did you think it was, the royal we?"

"I thought maybe it was one of those nurse things. I feel awful; do you feel awful?"

"Yes." He put his arm around her. "Where does it hurt?"

"I just ache all over, like somebody's been beating up on me."

"That's the fever. Go to sleep."

"Yes, Linc." She rolled over closer to him, to snuggle against his side.

He kissed her forehead. It felt as if it were on fire. "I'm sorry, poor baby," he said.

By the next day Linc's temperature was back to normal. Daisy's rose to 102 and stayed there, and Linc called the doctor, frantic with worry.

"If it goes higher, we'll hospitalize her," Dr. Banks said. "But she should be able to ride this out."

Hospitalize her.

He went upstairs and looked at her sweating in her

sleep. Daisy in a hospital. He crawled in bed beside her and held her, and she sighed and snuggled closer, still asleep, and he put his cheek on her hair and was afraid.

People called for Daisy.

Chickie was distraught, but Linc absolutely refused to let her in the house. "It's really contagious. She'd be frantic if she thought you might get it. You know how she feels about you."

"Oh, Linc." Chickie started to cry.

"I'll call you when the fever's gone," he promised. "You can come over and try to keep her in bed then." Chickie had to be content with that.

The kids were equally unhappy.

"Can't we just stand in the yard and wave to her through the window?" Andrew asked.

"She wouldn't recognize you. This is a bad fever. But I'll tell her you're all concerned. And I'll call you as soon as the fever's gone so you can all come back."

"That's really nice of you," Andrew said. "I know you're not crazy about having us all over there."

Linc felt as if he'd been hit. He searched for something to say. "Actually, I miss having you around. There are no cookies, and you've all spoiled Jupiter so rotten that he expects attention all the time. I'll call you the minute her fever breaks, trust me."

Bill called. "I heard about Daisy. This is rotten tim-
ing. I just found out that the little jerk I'd saved the
January show for has decided painting is no longer
his life. When she wakes up, tell her she's got that
show if she wants it. Even if she doesn't want it, actually. I'm in a bind here."

"She wants it," Linc said. "Go ahead, set it up. I'll
tell her as soon as she's lucid again."

Art came to the door, and Linc refused to let
him in.

"Just let me see she's all right." Art's face was
drawn with worry.

Linc felt a spurt of anger and then Art's obviously
real concern got to him. At least he got to see her; Art
wasn't even going to get that. "Look, I can't let you
in. The doctor is worried about this getting out. I
swear he comes to see her every day."

"Take care of her." Art looked at him with dis-
trust.

"I am," Linc said. "Believe me, I am."

He'd tried to sleep in his own room the first night,
but he was too worried about her, and when he finally
crawled into her bed and held her close, she slept better, without moaning or tossing, so he convinced himself that it was better that he stay with her and hold
her. In the few moments that she was lucid, she worried about him.

"You're so pale," she said weakly. "Are you eating?"

"Yes. Vegetable soup. Do you want some?"

But she'd eat only a little and then fall back into feverish dreams. Sometimes she'd cry out and then he'd hold her, wishing he knew what she was so afraid of so he could fix it. For the first time in his life, his schedule was completely disrupted and he was getting no work done, and he didn't care. When at the end of the week her temperature finally dropped, he was so relieved he walked around the house smacking his hand against the doorframes.

Midway through the week of her flu, Daisy got up in the middle of the night and went into the studio to paint. She'd been dreaming of Linc and of painting, dreaming of how much she loved him and wanted him, and of how much she wanted to paint in big, passionate strokes, of all the things she couldn't think about too much when she was healthy because she was afraid. The fever made her dizzy, but it also made her forget her fear, and she dragged one of the big canvases she'd stretched out of the corner and began to lay in charcoal lines for a portrait of Linc, blocking in his shoulders and his brow and jawline and his arms and hands. The next night she began to paint him, not in her usual meticulously detailed strokes, but in huge slashes of yellow and orange and red, full of strength and menace and passion and heat. She knew exactly what she was doing, and the fever drove her on. She painted for three nights straight while Linc slept exhausted from caring for her, and on the fourth night her fever broke.

She went into the studio and stared at the canvas. The portrait was huge and glowing and more sexual than she could ever have imagined herself painting; it was everything she'd thought about Linc and repressed, and if it felt good to have it all out, it was terrifying to look at it. She took the painting down from her easel and turned it against the wall, and put the other large canvas in its place.

You did it once sick, you can do it again healthy, she told herself, and began to draw on the canvas in charcoal, tentatively at first and then gradually using the same large, sweeping lines that she'd used to draw the first portrait. She loaded a four-inch brush with paint and laid on big patches of black and blue and gray and white, blocking in mass and light. When the dawn broke, she wiped the paint from her fingers and crawled back into bed.

• • •

"How are you?" Linc asked her when she woke at noon that day. He sat down beside her on the bed, holding a tray on his lap.

"I'm fine." Daisy leaned her head forward. "Feel."

He put his hand on her forehead, and all the tension went out of him when it was cool under his hand. He put the thermometer in her mouth. "If you're normal, you're well," he said, and then he laughed. Daisy was never normal.

When he took the thermometer out a minute later, she said, "That's not soup, is it?"

"Chicken noodle. Excellent for invalids. Ninety-eight point six. Good girl, Magnolia."

Daisy looked mulish. "I want a hamburger with onions and pickle and mustard and tomato."

"A hamburger? Daize, I don't think—"

Daisy set her jaw. "I want french fries. I want onion rings. I want a large, large Coke. I want a chocolate milk shake. I want a hot fudge sundae."

Linc started to laugh. "No. You'll get sick again. Start small. I'll go get you a hamburger and a Coke, and while I'm gone, you eat the soup."

"I don't want the soup." Daisy scowled.

When he was gone, she poured half the bowl of soup into the toilet and flushed away the evidence of her rebellion. Then she went into the studio.

The portrait of Linc stared back at her, roughed in

on the canvas, massive and brooding in gray and white and black. He looked powerful and cold and confident, the Linc she saw every day. The portrait was going to be terrific, she knew that just from the beginnings, and she couldn't decide why it depressed her so much. *You're just weak from the fever,* she told herself, and went back to bed to wait for her hamburger.

"Did you eat your soup?" Linc asked her when he got back, and she said, "No, I poured it in the john." She wolfed the hamburger, washing it down with the bubbly Coke with visible pleasure. When she handed him the empty paper cup, she said, "Now I feel like a real person again."

"You were always a real person. Don't get out of bed for a while. You were sicker than Mom and I, so it's going to take you longer. Sleep, so you don't have a relapse."

He waited until she'd obediently closed her eyes and he could hear her breathing slowly and steadily. Then he went downstairs to deal with the chaos left by their illnesses. They had bills, and yard work, and cleaning, and people coming to stay for Christmas in four days.

But when he looked into things, there was no chaos. Daisy had made a note of all the things she'd done while he was sick. She'd paid all the bills ahead of time. She'd sent the dry cleaning out, so all he had to do was pick it up. She'd made Christmas tree ornaments and left them in a box on the buffet. She'd hired Andrew to do the yard work, but when Linc called to ask him how much they owed him, Andrew refused to be paid.

"We all came over and did it together so it was done in a flash. Besides, we wouldn't take money from you. You're like family. When can we come back?"

"Come tomorrow," Linc said, touched. "I'll get a tree. We'll put Daisy on the couch to supervise and you all can decorate."

"Great," Andrew shouted. "Christmas cookies. Eggnog. There are still three of us here. We're not going home until Friday. Thank you. Oh, boy."

"Great," Linc said, not sure it was. "I'll get the tree."

But he didn't have to. Daisy had ordered a tree and evergreen swags and several bunches of mistletoe from a farmer who called to say he'd be delivering them that afternoon.

"Daisy already ordered a tree?"

"Yep, she ordered all this stuff a couple of weeks

ago. Said you were all gonna get the flu or something, and you wouldn't be around to do it yourselves. How are you?"

"We've all had the flu," Linc said through his amazement. "We're better now."

The grocery delivered Daisy's Christmas dinner order just as Linc hung up the phone with the farmer. A frozen turkey. Lots of bread for stuffing. Red and green sugar for Christmas cookies. Candy canes for the tree. Cranberry sauce.

What had happened to scatterbrained Daisy Flattery? Who was this woman who knew she was going to be sick and planned ahead for it? Not Daisy Flattery, who let the ravens feed her.

Daisy Blaise, he thought. *My wife. My wife, the adult.*

His throat closed with emotion, and he leaned against the stair post until he got his composure back. Then he heard her moving upstairs and went up to see if she was all right. She was throwing up her hamburger and Coke in the bathroom.

"I told you so," he said to his wife, the adult. "Now will you have some soup?"

The next day Andrew baked Christmas cookies while Linc and Olivia and Tracy struggled to get the tree straight. Daisy directed them from the couch, and they all finally decided that the tree was just crooked and there was nothing to be done about it.

"I like it better crooked." Daisy smiled at the tree and cuddled Liz happily. "It has more personality."

"Just what this house needed," Linc said. "More personality."

For tree trims, Daisy had woven little baskets of red and white gingham and filled them with bleached white baby's breath. She'd made stuffed doves of white velvet, and little stuffed pears of yellow velvet, stuffed gingerbread men and women of brown velvet trimmed in white rickrack and tiny round buttons. But as far as Linc was concerned, the best of the ornaments were quintessential Daisy, little hand-painted salt dough figures of all of them: Andrew in a chef's hat carrying his bowl of chocolate chip cookie dough, Lacey with a paintbrush wearing a dress covered in ivy, Olivia holding a women's history book and wearing an ERA T-shirt, Tracy sitting cross-legged tickling Jupiter, Evan looking gloomy as he looked at his apple, Julia holding her sides laughing, Bill holding canvases, Chickie beaming and clutching pink roses, Art with a stethoscope and small animals peeping out of all his pockets. Daisy had even done Booker and Crawford looking scholarly and Caroline carrying a microwave stuffed with books. They all looked rounder and cuter than in real life, like elves instead of realistic portraits, but Daisy had caught their personalities and the students were charmed.

"Take them home with you when you go," Daisy told them. "Merry Christmas from us."

Linc's figure had his typewriter under one arm and Jupiter under the other and he was wearing his letter jacket. He kept turning it in his fingers, fascinated by the detail. "How'd you know what the jacket looked like?"

"I found it in your stuff. I tried it on too. It's really warm."

Later, when they were all stuffing themselves with warm Christmas cookies and milk, he went upstairs and got the jacket. When he came down, he put it around Daisy's shoulders as she sat at the table.

"Stay warm," he said, and went into the kitchen so he wouldn't have to talk about it. When he came back out, she'd put her arms through the sleeves and was cuddled up in the jacket's yellow and black bulk, her dark hair tumbling over the huge shoulders like a molten waterfall.

"I want to know how to make these." Olivia turned her ornament over and over and marveled at the details, so Daisy told them how to mix the salt dough, and then showed them how to make the little sausage figures while Linc watched. It was all warm and comforting, like a family, and it made him a little nervous to be so warm and comforted, but he couldn't tear himself away.

The next day the students left, and Julia came into town. She stayed at the inn but spent every waking moment with Daisy. Evan began to haunt the house, which Linc didn't mind, and Art began to drop by every afternoon, which Linc did mind.

"What is he doing here?" he asked Daisy on Christmas Eve afternoon. "The party doesn't start until seven."

"He's a friend. Friends come by anytime."

"I should have told Caroline that," he said, and Daisy sniffed.

By eight the house was full of people who were full of good cheer and eggnog. The house looked like a *Better Homes & Gardens* photo spread, the Christmas dinner table looked like a Norman Rockwell magazine cover, and Daisy looked like a witch-queen in a long, low-cut green velvet dress she'd found at the secondhand clothing store in town. Linc knew it was secondhand because she'd told him when she'd crossed the hall to his bedroom to get help with the zipper. "It sticks," she said. "I think the last person who wore it jammed it." He'd eased the zipper up, watching the creamy flesh of her back disappear in the shortening V, noticing that she wasn't wearing a bra, using all his restraint to keep from reaching around and cupping her breasts. Since then she'd wrapped a thick red curtain rope around her waist and put holly in her hair, and Linc knew he should be wincing at how bizarre she looked, but he couldn't take his eyes off her.

"That holly should be mistletoe," he heard Art tell her at dinner, and she said, "That's in the hall."

Linc made a note to keep an eye on the hall. And an eye on Daisy. She was drinking a lot, he noted, finishing his own third cup of eggnog. He'd have to watch her.

"I cannot think who you remind me of." Daisy leaned precariously over Julia to see Evan. She was showing a lot of creamy cleavage, and Linc reminded himself to make a note to tell her not to bend over. "It's been driving me crazy ever since I met you." Daisy looked at Julia, who had a peculiar expression on her face. "Have you had too much eggnog, or do you know?"

"Both." Julia took Evan's hand in hers.

"Well, who?"

"Eeyore," Julia said.

"E. York?" Daisy echoed.

"No. Eeyore. From Winnie the Pooh."

"Oh, my God." Daisy fell back in her chair and laughed until she got the hiccups.

"Who's Eeyore?" Evan asked suspiciously.

"Absolutely my favorite childhood character." Julia looked into his eyes with drunken affection. "I loved Eeyore. I still do."

"Oh." Evan didn't pull his hand away. Linc resisted the urge to tell him there were probably germs on Julia's hand and poured himself another cup of eggnog. What the hell? He wasn't driving. Neither were they. Another great thing about Prescott: everybody lived within walking distance.

"I have ivy in my bathroom," Booker said to Linc. "I don't think I mind, but I'm constantly surprised when I go in there."

"Wait until she paints the snakes in." Linc shook his head at the thought. "There's one in my bathroom that stares at me while I wash my face."

"This is just perfect, honey," Chickie told Daisy. "This is the best Christmas I ever had."

"I love you, Chickie," Daisy said a little drunkenly. "I wish you weren't married to such a—"

"Christmas cookies in the living room," Linc said loudly. "Not to mention Lizzie Borden and her headless father. And there's a surprise for everyone on the Christmas tree. Could I see you in the kitchen for a minute, Daisy?"

"No." Daisy smiled lovingly at him and took his breath away. "But I'll be good."

Linc caught Art glaring at him. He glared back.

"Come on, Art." Daisy said just as brightly as Linc had a few moments before. "Linc, bring some more eggnog. Isn't this just lovely?"

Daisy put Christmas rock on the stereo and watched while everyone found his or her ornament, and the room became warm with laughter. Such nice people.

"Tell me what to do about Evan," Julia whispered in her ear. "I can't get him to make a pass."

"You're asking me? I'm *living* with a man who won't make a pass." Daisy watched her big, handsome husband talk to Evan and sighed. Then he looked up at her and smiled, and she felt heat all through her.

"Still?" Julia sounded drunkenly sympathetic. "What a waste. Now help me with Evan."

"I think you're just going to have to invite yourself home with him."

"What if he says no?"

Daisy snorted. "Evan is gloomy not insane. Besides, he's crazy about you."

"Yeah?"

"Yeah." Daisy grinned at her. "Go get him."

"Right." Julia squared her shoulders and marched across the room to her prey.

NINE

"WHAT AM I going to do about Julia?" Evan asked.

Linc looked around the room until he found Daisy. She was talking to Julia. Good. That meant she wasn't with the wife-stealing vet. He smiled at her and she smiled back, and he felt heat all through him. Evan was saying something.

"What?"

"Julia." Evan looked at Daisy's painting gloomily. "What do I do?"

"Ask her to come home with you. Offer to show her your etchings."

"I don't have any etchings."

Linc nodded. "Good. Julia probably hates etchings."

"Then why would she come?"

Linc couldn't help it; he started to laugh. "Because she wants you."

"Really?" Evan's face almost brightened. "How do you know?"

Linc thought about telling him how he knew when Julia was in the mood to go home with someone but decided not to. "Daisy told me. Daisy knows everything."

"This is true." Evan's eggnog was making him philosophical. "Sometimes I think that Julia and I could never be happy, and then I think of you and Daisy. If Daisy can make you warm, Julia can make me happy."

"I don't think anybody can make anybody else anything." Linc tried to be careful so he didn't get lost in his anys. "Daisy didn't make me warm."

Evan looked at him owlishly.

"What are you talking about?" Linc asked, irritated, and then Julia was beside them.

"I should probably start back to the inn." She looked at Evan and batted her eyes.

Here's your chance, old buddy, Linc thought, and nudged Evan.

Evan looked startled. "Oh?"

Linc closed his eyes and sighed. He liked Evan a lot, but sometimes—

"Is it dangerous to walk back to the inn alone?" Julia asked, still looking at Evan.

"Well—" Evan stopped, helpless.

Linc looked around for Daisy. This was obviously her kind of problem, getting two people together. Unfortunately, he couldn't find her. That bothered him. She was supposed to be there with him. He was going to have to find her and explain that to her, but first he had to take care of Julia and Evan.

"Yes, it's dangerous to walk back alone." Linc stopped to think. Just getting Evan to walk Julia home wasn't going to do it; he was going to have to actually get her into his apartment for the night. "But it's more dangerous at the inn," he said carefully. "You really shouldn't be staying there, Julia. The doors don't lock."

Julia looked at him with hopeless contempt. Well, he deserved it, that last bit had been feeble. He had to do better, but the eggnog was fogging his brain. What would Daisy say?

"They have rats," he said suddenly. "Big suckers. They've been known to carry off small children. You're small, Julia. An especially big rat might grab you. And there you'd be." He stopped. Where would she be? "Rat snacks."

"Rat snacks?" Julia looked incredulous.

Linc shook his head. "It would be terrible, just terrible." He drank some more eggnog.

They were looking at him as if he were insane. He'd seen the look before when Daisy had gone into one of her narrative fits in front of strangers. "So," he said, winding his story up in a hurry. "You really shouldn't be staying there. We'd let you stay here, but we don't have any room. So maybe you should stay somewhere else." He looked at Evan, who was looking like a bemused codfish. Julia, on the other hand, had the look of a woman on whom light had dawned.

Linc kicked Evan smartly on the ankle. "Have you got any room at your place, Evan?"

"Ouch," Evan said, and Julia said, "Would that be too much to ask, Evan, if I stayed with you?"

"What? Oh. No." Evan took a deep breath. "Absolutely not. My pleasure."

Linc sighed in relief and looked around to see if Daisy had come back. She hadn't.

"You know, being married to Daisy has taught you a lot," Julia said when Evan had gone for their coats. "She couldn't have done any better herself."

"Where is she?" Linc looked around the room

again. She was definitely gone. Julia said something, but he didn't hear.

There was mistletoe in the hall. *That damn vet,* Linc thought, and then stopped, confused. He should be delighted; Daisy finding someone else would get him off the hook permanently with Crawford. Not even Crawford could insist he hold on to a wife who was in love with someone else.

Just not the vet. He wasn't right for her. She needed someone who could give her a little structure, take care of her. Give her time and room to paint and—

Who are you kidding? he asked himself. The vet was perfect for her. He'd give her all the animals she wanted and would never yell at her because the furniture had holes or because she dressed funny. He should go do the right thing, tell them it was all right, that he'd give her a divorce, that they could be together. He thought of the vet basking in Daisy's glow and it hurt more than he could ever have imagined. But Daisy deserved the best. He put down his drink and went into the hall.

Art was kissing Daisy under the mistletoe.

The pain of losing her was suddenly much sharper, a twisting stab that was almost unbearable. He turned and went back into the living room and found his drink and drained it with one gulp. Then he went to get a refill.

• • •

Daisy looked up at Art and smiled ruefully. "I was really hoping you were the one." He should have been she knew; he was warm and funny and loved animals and didn't care about holes in the furniture or funny-looking clothes. But there had been nothing for her in his kiss. It had been a perfectly good kiss, but she felt more watching Linc smile at her across a room than she did when this lovely, sweet man kissed her. "I'm sorry." She took his hand. "I really thought I—"

Art shook his head. "But you don't."

"No," she said sadly. "And you're just the kind of man I should be perfectly happy with. I can't understand it."

"I can." He sighed. "You're in love with that gangster you married. God knows why."

Daisy tensed. "No. That's not it. I don't know what it is. But I feel awful for leading you on."

"You didn't." Art relaxed against the doorframe. "I knew it was too good to be true."

"You don't love me," Daisy said, making a new discovery. "That's good."

"No, but I could have. You're just the kind of woman I could be happy with." He looked down at her with affectionate bewilderment. "Am I still your vet?"

"Well, of course."

"Good. I'd miss having you around. But I am going to go now and think about rearranging my plans for the future. This sort of changes things for me." He kissed her on the cheek. "Merry Christmas, Daisy Blaise."

Daisy saw him to the door and watched him walk off into the snowy night. Art was the perfect man for her story and he was all wrong. The wrong man was back in the living room, and she knew he'd be perfect. Nothing made sense, so she went back to the archway into the living room to regroup. Julia and Evan had gone, she saw. Linc was saying good-bye to the Bookers, walking with them to the hallway, where she stood, and the Crawfords were following them. She looked at the clock. Midnight. The Cinderella hour. She sighed.

"Bye-bye, Daisy." Chickie held out her arms and Daisy went to give her a hug. "There," Chickie said with satisfaction, pushing her next to Linc. "You're under the mistletoe. Kiss her, Linc."

Daisy turned and found him looking down at her with such misery in his eyes that she was shaken. "What is it, love?" she whispered. She put her arms around him and pulled him to her for comfort and warmth, to drive away the misery inside him, and he held her so close she couldn't breathe. *This isn't close enough,* she thought. *I want you inside me.*

"Kiss her," Chickie insisted.

Daisy lifted her face and Linc bent to her, his body pressing hers, his hands warm on her back, and she felt her breath go, felt herself shake as his lips brushed softly against hers, and then she moved into his kiss and felt such heat and love shudder through her that she clutched at him, forgetting the Crawfords, forgetting everything but him, because he was so big and close and hot and because he was Linc, and Linc was all she had ever really wanted anyway.

When he broke the kiss, she put her head on his chest and hung on to him, so glad to have him finally in her arms that she almost wept with relief. She heard Chickie say something inane in the background, and then she felt Linc move his arm to catch the open door and shut it behind them, and then they were alone.

He put his hand under her chin and pulled her head up, and said, "Do you want a divorce?" His face was harsh and bleak. "Do you want Art Francis?"

"*No.*" Daisy shook her head and clung to him, clenching her teeth because she wanted him so much.

"I thought I did, but I was wrong. I told him so tonight. I want you. I've wanted you for so long. Will you *please* make love to me tonight? I can't stand living with you and not making love with you."

Something broke in his face, and he pulled her to him and kissed her so hard, she moaned a little against his mouth. Then his tongue invaded her, and she let go completely, letting her nails rake down his arms as she arched her body into his. He kissed her over and over again, not the polished kisses she'd expected from him, but rough, awkward, fumbling, hard kisses that left her mindless with love and lust. Her knees went weak and she tugged him down with her to sprawl on top of her on the hall carpet. His hands were hard on her waist, and she pulled one up to her breast and pressed it there while he pulled her hips close to his with the other, grinding his hardness into her until she wanted to scream. "I want you *now*," she told him, "*now*," and then she felt him yank on the zipper to her dress while she fumbled with his shirt buttons. His shirt finally came open, and she bit his chest, running her palms up his body while he groaned into her hair and yanked again at her stuck zipper.

She twisted against him, needing to be naked against him. "Rip it," she told him through her teeth.

"Rip it off." He slid his fingers into the neck of her dress, and she felt his fist against her breasts, felt his fingers slide into her cleavage, and she shuddered with bone-deep pleasure. Then he yanked hard on the old velvet and it split all the way down to her thighs, and the rush of cool air on her naked body was wonderful. Then his mouth was on her breast, and his hand stroked down her stomach and between her legs, sliding into her effortlessly because she needed him so much, and she screamed her relief as she clutched him to her and came.

Then he was kissing her again, and she bit his lip and said, "Inside me," and tried to find the zipper to his pants with shaking hands. He rolled away from her, capturing both her hands in his. "Upstairs," he said, and his voice was thick and hoarse. He stood and yanked her to her feet, and she let her arms fall so that her sleeves slipped off her arms, and her dress fell heavily around her hips, and she stood naked to the waist under the mistletoe.

Linc closed his eyes, and Daisy moved close against him, resting her cheek on his chest, letting her hands slide down his back so she could pull his hips to hers. He was so hard, and he felt so good against her. He pulled her dress and underwear down over her hips, his hands stroking hot down her waist until the weight of the velvet dropped everything to the floor. Then he picked her up and carried her up the stairs while she kissed and bit his neck and dug her fingernails into his arm, wanting him so much, she was mindless with it.

He tipped her back onto his bed and slid his fingers inside her again, and she struggled against his hand as the pressure rose in her. *"Inside me,"* she said again, and he stopped. She clutched at him, loving the heat and the hardness of his body, and he rolled against her, reaching over her to the bedside table. She barely had time to register that she really was in his bed with him—this time she really would have it all—before he had the condom on and had pulled her to him again.

Daisy looked up into Linc's eyes, so dark with need for her that they were almost black. "I thought I'd never have you like this," she told him. She eased herself under him, and he arched to let her, and when she wrapped her legs around him and pulled him to her, he closed his eyes and put his forehead on hers. "I've never wanted anyone like this," he told her. "Not like this." While she was savoring his words and his weight, he lifted his hips and moved into her, thick and hard, and Daisy lost everything in the heat as he thrust inside her, rolling so that she was on top, pulling her tighter to him. She clutched at him, licking her tongue into his mouth and he moaned her name, and his fingers dug into her back and arms while he moved like a madman inside her. He wasn't what she'd expected, wasn't the smooth, polished, controlled lover she'd thought he'd be, and knowing that he was going crazy in her arms because he was in *her* arms, knowing that it was Linc who was surging against her, whispering her name brokenly, telling her he loved her, knowing that it was Linc saying those mad, passionate things to her, all that made her crazy too. Her body went wild because Linc was so big and rough and hard inside her, but her mind pushed her over the edge because she knew it was Linc in her arms, inside her, and because she loved him so. He was so much, then too much, and the pressure built until it all exploded inside and she cried his name, and he rolled again and pinned her beneath him, stroking over and over as she writhed and sobbed mindlessly. Then he shuddered in her arms and dropped his head on her shoulder, whispering her name again and again.

"Stay with me," she whispered finally when all the shocks were gone and she was soft with satisfaction. "I want to sleep with you all night. I want to wrap myself around you all night."

"I couldn't ever leave you," he said into her hair. "I

couldn't ever let you go." And she fell asleep holding on to him and to his promise.

Daisy woke the next morning in the wrong bed with the right man. Linc pressed against her back, warm and naked, his hand still curved around her breast, and she closed her eyes for a moment because he felt so good. Then she put her hand over his and pressed it against her breast, and he stirred and kissed her hair.

"It's Christmas," she said, and he laughed and said, "It sure is." He rolled away a little and pulled her onto her back, and he was beautiful in the morning sunlight. He ran his hand up to her neck to cradle her face, and then he kissed her. "Merry Christmas, Daisy Blaise."

Daisy snuggled against him, resting her cheek on his chest, still amazed that she finally had him naked in bed with her. "It's so warm with you," she said, and he said, "That's you. It's always warm wherever you are."

"No." Daisy raised herself up a little on one elbow so she was nose to nose with him. "I was really cold without you. You heat things up considerably." She kissed him on the nose, and then on the lips, and then started down his neck. After months of wanting him, she wasn't going to waste a minute.

"Your Christmas present's under the tree," Linc said, and his voice was breathless but happy. "You keep this up, you won't get it for hours."

Daisy stopped and grinned up at him, her chin resting on his stomach. "You're right." She rolled out of bed and headed for the stairs. *I'll ambush him under the tree.*

"Hey," he said and reached for her, but she grabbed her lace robe and ran downstairs.

Linc grabbed a condom from the bedside table and went downstairs to seduce his wife. He found her cross-legged in front of the tree. Her warm skin showed through the lace of her robe and he wanted her; it was a very familiar, frustrating ache, and he'd automatically begun to fight it when he realized that he didn't have to, that he had her, she was his, and if he went up and put his arms around her, she'd melt into him and they'd make love, and he'd never be cold again. He felt amazed and relieved and terrified and turned on all at the same time, and when he started to go dizzy, he took a deep breath and sat down beside her.

She was trying to rattle a very small package, but when he sat beside her, she stopped and tore off the wrappings. Inside were earrings he'd sent for from the jewelry store in Pennsylvania, pearl and sapphire daisy earrings quivering on almost invisible gold wires, and he watched her face light up, and thought she was the most beautiful woman he'd ever seen.

"Oh, Linc, they match my ring," she said, and turned to smile at him and took his breath away.

"I thought they'd be pretty against your hair." He touched one of her springy curls where it lay against her robe, and then let his hand do what it had wanted to do a thousand times since he'd met her, thread itself through her hair and pull her head back. Her lips parted as she felt the tug, and she let her head fall back against his hand and gave herself up to him, and he kissed her, slipping his tongue into the sweetness of her mouth and letting himself melt into her.

"Thank you," she whispered against his mouth, and then she smiled. "Wait, I have to try these on." She stood and went to the hall mirror and put the earrings on, and he felt bereft, watching her touch them with her fingertip to see them sparkle as they moved, so far away from him. "They're the most beautiful things I've ever owned," she called back to him, "next to my ring, of course."

He followed her and put his arms around her from behind, feeling his throat catch as she relaxed into him. He looked at her in the mirror; she was fresh and glowing, her eyes huge and dark. "You're so beautiful."

"That's contentment." Daisy laughed, and Linc felt her laughter against his body. "Hey," she said, and tried to move away. "There was another box under there for me in your writing. Let go."

"That's nothing." He felt embarrassed and held her tighter. "Really nothing."

"Ha." She squirmed out of his arms and went back to the tree, and he followed her again, feeling stupid because of the second present.

It was just a salt dough angel, except not very well made because he'd had to do it himself, clumsily topping it with curly dark hair and putting a paintbrush in its hand, dressing it in a yellow dress that went almost to its ankles. It looked stupid when she'd unwrapped it and sat holding it, not saying anything. "You didn't make one for yourself." Linc felt awkward. "It's such a dumb gift, but I felt bad that you didn't have one and there was some dough stuff left over after the kids left."

"Thank you," she said quietly, and when he looked at her, she was crying, and he didn't know what to do. She took a hook from the tree and hung the angel next to the Linc ornament. "This is my best Christmas ever," she told him, and then she hid her face against his chest. He wasn't sure what to do, so he just held her, and when she finally lifted her face to his, and he kissed her, she kissed him back with such passion and love that he lost his breath. She pulled him down underneath the tree, and the smell of the evergreen mingled with the perfume of her hair, and he barely remembered to wait until he'd pulled the condom from his robe pocket before he gave himself up to her and she loved him until he lost his mind. When he had his breath back, he laughed into her neck because he was so happy and so much in love with her.

"Hey," she whispered, her voice thick with satisfaction. "What's so funny?"

"Nothing." He kissed her hard, and then pulled her over on top of him so that his weight was off her, wincing as he felt the hard, cold floor under him. "We have two beds upstairs. We really should use them sometime. Not that I'm complaining, but these damn wood floors are hell on my knees." He held her close, balanced on top of him, kneading his fingers into the lace on her back, and he tried to be nonchalant about the fact that he couldn't bear to let her go.

"Poor baby." Daisy flicked her tongue over his

lips. She stretched lazily on top of him and then looked up and froze. "Oh, no."

"What's wrong?" He spilled her off him as he rolled to see what she was looking at, but he kept his arms around her to hold her close.

Jupiter was sitting in the doorway to the hall, staring at them with his one good eye, his tongue lolling out of the toothless side of his mouth. While they watched, his bad hip gave out, and he slid over onto one side on the polished wood floor and lay there like a drunken odalisque.

"He watched." Daisy put her head on Linc's shoulder, overcome. "We've probably scarred him for life. He'll never have a normal sex life now. Other dogs will be interested in him, attractive dogs, sweet, kind, caring dogs, dogs that could fill his life with intense physical pleasure, but no. No, Jupiter will never be able to accept the love of any other dog because of this traumatic Christmas morning."

I am the luckiest man on the face of the earth, Linc thought, but all he said was "Jupiter's been neutered."

"You have no imagination," Daisy said.

He wiggled his eyebrows at her. "Want to bet? Get the chocolate syrup and the vacuum cleaner and meet me upstairs." Daisy laughed, and he pulled her close to feel her body shudder with her laughter. "I love you, but you're corrupting me. I told a story last night to get Julia into Evan's bed."

Daisy's mouth dropped open, and then she grinned. "Julia slept with Evan?"

Linc snorted. "How should I know? Julia went home with Evan. I'd say it's a fifty–fifty chance."

She tightened her grip on him as her smile widened. "What kind of story? Tell me. Nobody ever tells me stories."

"Big rats at the inn. It sounded better with eggnog." Linc fell into her smile again and suddenly wanted her again. And he could have her. This was such an amazing thought that he kissed her until she was breathless and then pulled her to her feet. "Come with me, Magnolia. There are condoms upstairs I want you to meet."

"Your present's up there too." Daisy smiled at him over her shoulder as she headed for the stairs.

"Good. Get the syrup."

"No, a real present. Making love isn't a present."

"It is if you do it right. We do it right."

"Yes, we do, but that's not it."

She took him into the studio. "I finished it yesterday morning," she said, and he stood, amazed.

The Linc in the portrait was solid, and strong, and successful, massive in bluish tones of black, white, and gray. He was turning, his right shoulder a mass of charcoal gray, his left a block of black, broken only by the slashes of grayed white that suggested strong hands holding an open book. But it was his face, rising out of the monolith that Daisy had painted as his body, that was riveting. She'd sculpted the planes of his face so they were strong and brooding, and his eyes were lit with intelligence. It was the portrait of a statesman, the portrait of a man of learning, the portrait of a man of substance and worth and intelligence and power. "Is this how you see me?" he asked, flattered beyond words.

"Well, it's part of you." Daisy glanced toward a canvas that was turned to the wall. "I'm sorry it's so cold."

He cupped her face in his hands and said, "It's magnificent," and then he kissed her.

I'll tell him about the other one later, Daisy thought, and then she just thought about Linc.

Julia came over in the afternoon for leftovers, and Daisy lured her into the kitchen with a request for her to carry things to the table.

"So you stayed at Evan's last night." Daisy pulled the plate of cold turkey from the refrigerator.

"Yes." Julia grinned, remembering. "There are giant rats at the inn. I had to."

Linc came in and picked up the platter of cold turkey. "Hi, Julia," he said, and then he kissed Daisy full and hard on the mouth before he went into the dining room.

"Oh?" Julia said when he was gone.

"There were giant rats in his bedroom." Daisy pulled the potatoes and gravy out of the refrigerator to hide her own grin. "So he had to sleep with me. Is Evan any less depressed?"

"No." Julia found the cookies and bit into one. "He thinks I'll forget him when I go back to Pennsylvania. Do you have any tea? These cookies need tea."

"Will you forget him?"

"Maybe."

Daisy stopped shoving food into the microwave and turned around. "You're kidding."

Julia stood up and went to the cupboard. "He was very sweet, and I had a very good time, truly, it was lovely, but I don't think he's the one either."

Daisy blinked at her as she began to search the cupboards for tea. "That's not the way the story is supposed to end. Didn't Linc tell it right?"

"He told it right." Julia stopped and grinned as she remembered. "You should have heard it. Rat snacks." Then her grin faded. "It just wasn't my story. I don't think anybody can tell your story but you, you know?" She found the tin marked cocoa and took it down. "Would you hurry up with the gravy so we can nuke the potatoes? I'm starving." Julia found the cocoa tin and opened it. "Daisy?"

Daisy pulled the potatoes out of the microwave. "What?"

"This cocoa tin is full of cocoa."

"Amazing." Daisy put the gravy in the microwave and swung the door shut. "What'll they think of next?"

"You've changed," Julia said.

Daisy leaned against the counter as the microwave hummed behind her. "Well, I had to. Linc couldn't stand the chaos, and it's not that big a deal."

"When was the last time you told a story?" Julia asked her. "I haven't heard you tell one for months. Not since you got married."

"I told one this morning," Daisy said. "To Linc. About Jupiter."

"And before that?"

Daisy thought back. "I haven't had much time," she said, ignoring the little chill Julia's questions were starting. "I've been painting. Really good stuff." She thought about the bright painting of Linc that she'd turned against the wall and felt guilty, and then she realized she was feeling guilty about her best work, and the chill grew.

"Daisy, this isn't good," Julia said, and the microwave dinged, and Daisy pulled the gravy out with pot holders and handed it to Julia.

"This goes in the dining room," she said.

"Daisy—"

"Stay out of my story, Julia," Daisy said. "I'm really happy, so happy I can't believe it, and I'm willing to pay a lot for that. It's my story."

Julia nodded. "All right. But I miss the way you used to be."

"Julia says Evan's not going to work out for her," Daisy told Linc when Julia was gone.

"Very picky woman, Julia," Linc said.

Daisy frowned. "I know, I can't believe she dumped you. Which reminds me, did you ever do the chocolate syrup and vacuum cleaner bit with Julia?"

"I never took a major appliance anywhere near Julia. And since I never touched sugar until you moved into my life, I certainly never syruped her either. Do we have any Christmas cookies left?"

"I've ruined you," Daisy said complacently. "They're in the cookie jar. I want some too. We are out of chocolate syrup, however."

"Well, make a note to get some." Linc kissed her.

"This sex stuff can get boring if you don't stay innovative."

"Right." Daisy smiled at him and he sighed.

"Forget the syrup. The day I'm bored with you is the day I have no pulse." Jupiter pawed at his leg and he looked down. "Who taught this dog to beg? This is disgusting."

He fed Jupiter some turkey, and Daisy loved him so much, she thought her heart would break. *This is worth everything,* she thought, and pushed Julia's questions out of her mind.

Linc came home late one day in January a week before Daisy's gallery show and found her sitting at the bottom of the stairs, her face pale with shock. He dropped his briefcase and went to her, pulling her close to him. "What is it? What's wrong?"

"It's my father," she said dully. "My mother wrote him about the show. She was so proud I finally did something he'd like that she wrote him to brag about it. He's coming. With my stepmother. And my stepsisters. He wants to meet you. He's heard about your book." She took a deep breath and looked at him. "He approves of me. After all these years." She sounded bitter and hurt and Linc wanted to kill her father.

"The hell with him. Write and tell him not to come."

"No." She swallowed. "You have to meet him sometime. And if they come during the show, we'll be too busy to have to spend much time with them. This is best."

Linc took the letter from her and read the typewritten lines. It was cold and impersonal and ended with the hope that she had matured over the years and that her new husband, a man respected in his field, had had a beneficial influence on her appearance and behavior.

"Your father's a jerk." He threw the letter in the hall wastebasket. "Stick with Pansy."

"That's what I've done all my life." Daisy stared dully at the door in front of her. "I have to face him sometime. He's my father." She got up and walked upstairs, and Linc watched her go, helpless to ease her hurt.

I will never shut my child out like that, he thought, and realized that it was the first time he'd ever thought about a real child, not some well-pressed fantasy. A curly-headed baby with Daisy's smile. He thought about following her up the stairs and suggesting they start one now, but he knew it was too soon. After this show was over and their lives were back to normal, he and Daisy were going to have to do some serious talking about their future. But not now. She had enough to think about with her show and her father.

He went in and found her sitting on the edge of their bed, and he put his arms around her and pulled her down onto the comforter with him, and she said, "I love you like nothing else in this world." And he comforted her.

Daisy made Julia go shopping with her for a dress for her opening at Bill's gallery. Then over Julia's protests, she bought a plain, high-necked black linen dress with fitted sleeves that made her look chic and adult.

"That dress is not you." Julia crossed her arms and scowled. "You've never worn anything that conservative in your life. I saw a boutique down the street. They had tie-dyed chiffon. Let's go."

"No." Daisy admired her black starkness in the mirror. "I look like a real person in this. Not even my father could complain about this. This is something Caroline would wear."

Julia made a face. "Why would you want to wear what she'd wear? She's so conservative, she doesn't wear colors." Then Julia saw the light. "Ah. Just like

Linc. Daisy, you dummy, Linc likes you in colors. You don't have to dress like him."

Daisy turned sideways in the mirror. The black made her look slender. Sophisticated. Serious. "This is a real dress for a real adult. I'm buying it."

"That's the most boring dress I've ever seen," Julia said flatly, but Daisy bought it anyway. It made her look like Daisy Blaise, and that was all that mattered.

TEN

Daisy threw up the night of the opening. She sat on the bathroom floor in black lace underwear and shuddered with fear. All those people. Her paintings. Her father. She'd been so paralyzed with fear for the past week that she hadn't painted. Bill had come over with a couple of his employees to pick up her work, and she'd told him that her paintings were in the studio. Then she'd sat down on the couch and put her head between her knees.

"Nerves," Bill had said. "Happens a lot. Leave it to me. I'll get everything." And he had, even the collages from the hall. He'd even come back to take pictures of the cherubs in the bathroom and the trompe l'oeil in the kitchen. Everything she had ever done was going to be at this show. She felt naked when she thought about it.

Pull yourself together, she lectured herself. *Be an adult. You're acting like Daisy Flattery. Grow up.* Right. She stood and brushed her teeth. There was something about brushing your teeth that was civilizing. Very Daisy Blaise. She tried to tell herself a story about Daisy Blaise, about her hugely successful gallery show and even more successful marriage, but it didn't work. Daisy Blaise was reality, and the show could flop, and her marriage was wonderful but asked her to be something she wasn't, and she wasn't sure she could cope much longer, and—worst of all— she couldn't make a story about it.

When she left the bathroom, Linc was waiting on the landing.

Daisy was wearing something that looked like a black lace bathing suit that didn't have a bottom, and she had on black bikinis underneath it, and Linc felt dizzy just looking at all that black lace on the body he loved. "Well, that's interesting," he said. "How does it come off?"

"Hooks." Daisy moved past him into the bedroom. "Lots of hooks. You can play with it after the show."

Linc moved into the doorway and watched her slip

on her stockings, smoothing them over her full calves and thighs. "I may not be able to wait until after the show. Have I ever told you how beautiful you are?"

"All the time." She smiled up at him faintly. "Usually I'm undressed when you mention it."

"That's because every time I get near you, I undress you."

"I love you." She stopped fumbling with her garters and looked up at him, and her voice was intense. "I really love you. More than anything or anyone. I'll be anything you need me to be."

Linc tried to pull himself out of the haze the black lace had brought on. She was telling him something important here, and he wasn't getting it. "I don't need you to be anything but Daisy Blaise." Her face crumpled a little, so he moved to the bed and pulled her onto his slap. "Don't be scared, Magnolia. Everything's going to go fine tonight. You're a terrific painter, and after tonight everybody will know that."

"I know." Daisy scrambled off his lap. "Wait until you see this dress."

He watched her bend over to finish her garters and felt the buzz return. "I'm already crazy about the underwear."

Daisy pulled on a black lace slip, smoothing it over her hips, and he wanted to help her. Then she jerked a dress off the hanger and pulled it over her head, turning her back to him so he could zip her up. It was depressing watching all that warm flesh and black lace disappear as he eased the zipper up, but what went up would come down again, and he could wait.

Then she turned and held out her arms to show him the dress. "What do you think?"

Linc had spent a lot of time with a lot of women, and he wasn't stupid. "You look great," he said, but he thought, *What the hell is she doing in a dress like that? It looks like something Caroline would wear.*

"Good." Daisy turned to her mirror. "I think I look adult and respectable."

"Absolutely," Linc said. She did look adult and respectable. He hated it. "You ready to go?"

"I'll be right down." She picked up her brush and started on her hair.

"What are you doing?"

"My hair. Go on. I'll be down in a minute."

Linc left, feeling very uneasy, and he felt worse when she came downstairs. She'd pulled her hair back into a tight knot on her neck. The black velvet bow that kept her curls imprisoned framed her face like black wings. She looked pale and forbidding and cold and unhappy.

"Daisy," he began, and then stopped. It was her night. If that was the way she wanted to look, that was the way she could look. "Let's go, Magnolia. You look great."

The gallery was full when they got there, and Bill grabbed Linc as he and Daisy walked through the door. "Where have you been?"

Linc jerked his head at Daisy, who had moved past them and into the gallery. "Nerves. Don't say anything. She's terrified."

Bill squinted at her and frowned. "Why is she dressed like Morticia Addams?"

"I don't know." Linc spread his arms helplessly. "She's been nuts for a couple of weeks now. I can't wait until this is over and things go back the way they were."

"Don't count on it." Bill grinned at him. "Daisy's a hit. We're almost sold out already. I've had a couple of offers on your portraits too. Huge offers. Will you sell?"

"My portrait? Absolutely not." Linc grinned, remembering Christmas. "It was my second-best Christmas present."

"The first one must have been a beauty," Bill said. "How about the other one?"

"What other one?"

"Whichever one isn't your present. I know they're a set, but I can still find a buyer for one."

"There was another portrait?"

Bill jerked his thumb to the back wall, and Linc turned to see where he pointed.

His black-and-white portrait was there, and in that one he still looked distinguished, intelligent, and powerful. But next to it was one done in yellow and orange, a mirror image to the cold gray portrait. Instead of a gray-suited body, Daisy had painted him in the nude, in fluid slashing strokes, laying in the flat muscular planes of his body in hot slabs of paint that glowed on the canvas. It was as abstract as the first painting, and thank God, the torso ended at the bottom of the canvas, just above his hips, but he was undeniably naked. The face was the worst part. It was him, all right, but all the dignity of the first portrait had been replaced with passion and heat. She'd picked out the lights in his eyes and hair with red, and he flamed on the canvas. He was distinguished, intelligent, and powerful in the first painting, but in this one he was passionate, seething, and erotic. If he'd seen it in the privacy of her studio, he'd have made love to her on the floor under it because she saw him like this. In the glare of the gallery, with everyone in Prescott looking at him, he wanted to kill her.

Julia came up beside him. "You never looked like that with me."

Julia was the last thing he needed. "Shut up."

She stepped back. "You can't possibly be upset about this. That is a great painting."

"Well, when she paints you in the nude, we'll hang it here too."

"She can paint me in the nude anytime she wants." Julia frowned at him. "I thought you'd loosened up."

He couldn't take his eyes from the portrait. Imagine when Crawford saw it. "I am never going to get that loose."

"Guess what!" Daisy materialized out of the crowd, bouncing with joy. "Bill just showed me the sales slips. He's sold almost everything. I'm a hit. Isn't that wonderful? Why are you frowning."

He turned to glare at her. "I don't like surprises."

"What surprises?" Daisy scowled at him, back to her normal self. "What's wrong?"

"The other portrait." Linc nodded to the back wall, almost too angry to speak.

Daisy turned around, and he watched the color drain from her face. "That wasn't supposed to be here. That was private."

"Then how did it get here?"

"Bill must have found it. I told him he could have anything in the studio. I forgot. I was nervous and I forgot." She turned back to him, bloodless with panic.

Linc closed his eyes. "You forgot. How the hell could you forget something like that?"

"Linc." Daisy's voice was desperate. "I'm sorry. I'm really, really sorry."

"I know you're sorry." His voice was cold, and he watched as she winced under his words as if they were slaps, so angry he didn't care. "But I'm the one who has to face these people. I have *students* here."

"I'm sorry." Her voice was so low, he could barely hear her.

"We'll talk about it later." He turned away and came to face-to-face with an older man of about his height and coloring. "Excuse me." Linc pushed past him and walked away.

"Well, Linc, my boy." Crawford caught him, frowning as he jerked his head toward the portraits. "Not quite the image I had of you."

Here we go. "Well, sir, Daisy sees a different side of me."

"I think it's lovely." Chickie held on to her drink for dear life and beamed at Linc. "Daisy's so talented. You must be very proud."

"Shut up, Chickie," Crawford said savagely. "You don't know squat. That dumb woman may have wrecked his career with that piece of porn."

Chickie buried her face in her glass, and Linc stopped thinking about himself and thought about what an ass Crawford was. "It's not pornography. Daisy's an artist. She—" He broke off when he saw Crawford stare past his shoulder. He turned and found Daisy beside him with the older man he'd passed before at her side. Beyond him was a thin, elegantly dressed older woman and two younger carbon copies, all with disappointed mouths and thin eyebrows.

Daisy was blue-white pale, and her eyes were like coals. "Chickie, Linc, Dr. Crawford, this is my father, Gordon Flattery, my stepmother, Denise Flattery, and my stepsisters, Melissa and Victoria." She drew a deep breath. "Dr. Crawford is dean of liberal arts here, Father. And Chickie Crawford arranged my wedding. It was beautiful." She smiled at Chickie with tears in her eyes. Chickie smiled back just as woefully.

"Dr. Crawford." Gordon Flattery shook hands firmly while he and Crawford nodded eye to eye. "Lincoln." Linc's hand was also firmly pressed. "Mrs. Crawford." Chickie got a dignified nod. "I'm pleased to meet you all."

Crawford's frown smoothed out a little as he recognized a kindred spirit, and Linc wanted to dump his drink on both of them. *Self-satisfied stuffed shirts.*

Chickie looked back at the yellow portrait. "You

must be proud of your daughter. Such beautiful paintings."

Flattery frowned. "Well, she's certainly matured in appearance from the ragbag she used to be." He looked at Daisy's black dress with qualified approval, and she stiffened, no longer teary. Linc watched Daisy's chin come up and her scowl harden her face, and he thought, *Good, stand up to him. I don't want you to care what he thinks.* Then she turned and looked at him the same way, and he flinched. *Wait a minute—*

"But I'm not sure about her artwork." Daisy's father looked back at the yellow portrait too, and then turned to Linc. "I can't think what you were doing, letting her show that thing."

"Exactly what I was telling him." Crawford expanded. "Daisy may not have been smart enough to know that sort of thing wouldn't do, but I expected more of Linc."

"Linc didn't know." Daisy's voice was flat but firm. "He's as appalled as you are."

Linc started to speak, but Flattery overrode him.

"What were you thinking of, Daisy? He has to face these people. His *students* are here."

Linc stopped breathing, stunned by the echo of his own words.

"I was thinking of Linc." Daisy took a deep breath

and went on. "I was thinking of both sides of him, and I wanted to paint him, and I did, and I think it's my best work, and I'm not sorry." She turned and met Linc's eyes, angry and miserable and lost but defiant. "I'm not sorry at all. That's a beautiful portrait, and you should be proud that you're like that." She bit her lip. "I'm proud you're like that, like both of them."

Chickie's drink had made her bold. "I think so too. I think they're both beautiful."

"I told you to shut up." Crawford looked at Chickie with contempt. "You're as dumb as Daisy."

"Why don't you leave him?" Daisy told her passionately. "He's a terrible person. He's always making passes at other women, and he treats you like dirt. Leave him."

In the shocked silence that followed, Linc looked at all the people gathered around him and realized that he really gave a damn about only one of them, and it was time he said so, but not until Daisy had her say. He was done trying to stifle Daisy.

Crawford found his voice and said, "That's about enough," but Chickie said, "Where would I go?"

Daisy stuck out her chin. "You can come live with me. I'm leaving, so I don't know where that will be exactly, but you can come with me. Leave him. You're too good for him. The only reason you drink too much is because he makes you so miserable."

Chickie looked at the glass in her hand as if she were seeing it for the first time. Then she put it down on the nearest table and walked away.

Crawford seethed. "Listen, you—"

"No." Linc stopped him cold. "You cannot talk to my wife in that tone of voice." Daisy turned to follow Chickie, and he caught her arm as he finished with Crawford. "And if you ever touch Daisy again, not only will I break your fingers, I will report you to the board of regents for sexual harassment. And I'll be damned if I know why I've waited four months to tell you that, you old goat."

Crawford dropped his drink. *"What?"*

Linc ignored him to face Daisy's father. "I'm very proud of Daisy's work, and you're a fool if you can't see how talented she is. Everyone else who's here can. The only mistake she made tonight is that damned dress she has on, and she wore that for you and me." He looked down at Daisy. "Don't do that again. You look weird when you get this conservative."

Daisy scowled at him. "Listen, you don't have to do this—"

"Come here." He pulled her away from the idiots and through the crush of people and into Bill's office at the back of the gallery, and she tripped along behind him, her hand cold in his. When they were inside the dark office, lit only by the faint light from the single window, he said, "First of all, you can forget about moving. Chickie can have my bedroom, but you're staying." Then he turned her around and unzipped her dress, enjoying the way her flesh and the black lace came back to him.

Daisy tried to move away. "Wait a minute, what are you doing?"

"What I should have done before we came." He jerked the dress over her head, peeling it over her arms as she struggled to keep it on. When he had it off, he walked over to the window, opened it, and threw the dress out into the alley.

"Linc!" Daisy went after it, and he caught her. He pulled the bow out of her hair and ran his fingers through her curls until they were as free and full as before, and then he kissed her. "I love you," he told her. "I screwed up out there for a minute, but I'm smarter now, and I love you. You, not whoever was wearing that damn dress." And then he kissed her again, harder, trying to bring her back to life, the way it worked in fairy tales.

His mouth was hot on hers, and Daisy gave up trying to argue with him and just leaned into his heat. It felt so good to be out of that awful dress, and even better to be back in his arms. The heat flared in her and she wanted him again, the way she always did, and it was like coming home. "I thought you'd never hold me like this again," she whispered into his jacket.

"I'm dumb, but I'm not that dumb." He kissed her hair, and her forehead, and her nose, and then her lips, and she laughed until she felt his mouth on her throat and then her breast, and she wanted to give herself up, but there was still too much between them.

She pulled away from him until his eyes came up to meet hers. "I have to tell you, that portrait being here is probably a by-mistake-on-purpose deal." He frowned with confusion, and she tried again. "I think I told Bill to take everything in the studio because deep down inside I wanted to people to see the Daisy Flattery part of me. I think the Daisy Flattery part of me just couldn't take being squelched anymore, you know?"

"I know." Linc put his arms around her again. "I think the Daisy Flattery part of me is what threw the dress out the window."

Daisy smiled into his chest, but she had to make sure he understood. "Listen, I'm not ashamed of who I am even if I am weird. And I'm not ashamed of that portrait."

"I'm not either." Linc held her tighter. "Anytime I'm feeling depressed, I'm going to go look at it and think, *This is what Daisy thinks of you.* And then I'm going to jump you." He bent to kiss her, and she felt dizzy and relieved and turned on, right in the middle of Bill's gallery. And she didn't have any clothes. "Linc, what am I going to wear home?"

"I don't care. Your slip's nice." He slid his hand over her breast and inside the slip, and she gave up and pressed against him, but then the door opened.

"I know you wanted to be alone with Daisy," Julia said, squinting into the darkness from the bright gallery. "But if you're yelling at her, I'm against it."

"He threw my dress out the window." Daisy pulled away from Linc before Julia saw. "He messed up my hair and threw my dress away."

"Good. That dress stunk on ice." Julia turned to go.

"Get her coat, please." Linc pulled Daisy close again in the darkness, sliding his hand down her back to her rear end, pulling her even tighter until she felt how hard he was, and she closed her eyes with pleasure. "She's shy about walking around in her slip. Also, we're going home."

"Why?" Julia stopped in the open doorway. "The party's just started and it's great. This is Daisy's big moment. You can't go home now."

Linc's hands moved over Daisy in the dark, and his hips pulsed into hers, and Daisy couldn't talk.

Linc could. "We have things we need to discuss."

Julia snorted. "If they're the usual things you want to discuss with Daisy, this door has a lock."

She closed the door behind her when she went, and Linc reached over and flipped the lock closed. Then he turned back to Daisy. "Show me where the hooks are on this Merry whatsit."

"Widow." Daisy fought her way through a fog of lust. "Listen, we can't do this here; my *father's* out there."

Linc slid his hands up her thighs and grabbed the bottom of her slip. "That's not a father. That's a sperm donor. Forget him. He's a mess. Concentrate on me. I'm terrific."

He pulled her slip over her head, and Daisy shivered at the impact of the cool air and Linc's hands and felt wonderful. "Pretty sure of yourself, aren't you?"

"Yes." Linc's voice was thick with confidence and lust, and he trapped her against Bill's desk without hesitation, pressing himself into her until she breathed harder and deeper. "Forget playing hard to get, cupcake. I've seen the pictures you painted of me. You think I'm God." He found the hooks and started undoing them, flipping them open while he bore down on her, and his fingers felt so good against her skin that she gave up even pretending to fight him and let the heat sweep over her, and she thought, *I have it all,* and then she thought only about him.

Later, dressed in her black coat, Daisy floated through the throng of people, smiling at everyone, buoyed up by the admiration for her work and wrapped in the sure knowledge of Linc's love. Crawford was livid, her father was disgusted, and her stepmother was supercilious, and Daisy didn't care. She thought her stepsisters looked envious. Then she looked at Linc and thought, *No wonder.* It really was better being Cinderella than the stepsisters. You just had to hang on until the happy ending.

She was gone when Linc woke up the next morning, and he panicked for a minute before he found her note on the bedside table: "Gone to see Chickie. Back by eleven. Love, Daisy."

Love, Daisy.

He put the note in his drawer and got dressed, and took Jupiter out on the lawn and carefully threw sticks for him. And all the while he thought about Daisy and about Daisy's father.

He could have been that man. If Daisy hadn't loved him, he could have been like that. Daisy had saved him, and he had almost ruined her. She'd worn that awful dress for him. And last summer he would have thought it was great. Thank God he'd changed.

Olivia and Andrew came by, oddly cautious. "Is Daisy home?"

Linc smiled at them and waved them to sit down. "She'll be back soon."

They sat down to wait, and Andrew threw a stick for Jupiter, but Andrew was sloppy and it landed on Jupiter's blind side, so he sat and looked dopey until Andrew went to show him the stick.

"We really can't stay too long." Olivia seemed edgy. "We just came to show her this."

This was a record album with a picture of five leering musicians on the front. One of them looked vaguely familiar.

"Could Daisy have known these guys?" Olivia's voice was cautious.

"Daisy knows everybody." Linc took the album. "Why?"

"There's a song on here." Olivia blushed. "The lyrics are inside. We'd better go." She stood up and yelled for Andrew, and they walked off together.

Linc pulled the lyrics sheet out and skimmed through it until he came to a song called "Daisy Paradise." The song was explicit, about making love with a dark-haired woman who had a body made for sinking into until the singer died of satisfaction. Linc turned the album back over. The one who'd looked familiar was Derek. He'd made his album.

Linc leaned his head back against the porch pillar and thought about throttling Daisy, and then sanity returned. If any of his ex-lovers ever took up rock, he'd be in the same boat. And anyway, this kind of thing was standard fallout from loving Daisy. There'd be other things in the future that would embarrass him if he stayed with her, so he'd either have to give her up or get used to it.

And giving her up was out of the question.

He thought about Daisy, about everything that exasperated him about her, about everything that disappointed her about him, about everything that made her Daisy, and then he left to make some changes.

When Daisy came home at eleven, she parked the Nazimobile behind a red four-wheel-drive sport van.

"Whose car is that?" she asked as she came up the walk, and then she stopped.

Linc was sitting on the porch steps with Liz, Annie, and Jupiter. The animals were wearing bright red collars, and Annie screeched her hello, and Jupiter barked and fell off the porch, and Liz opened one eye and then closed it. Linc wore a bright red sweater that matched.

"Color." Daisy shook her head, blinded by the red.

"Come here." Linc reached for her, and Daisy stepped back. "Linc, this is the front porch. People can *see*."

"Good. Let 'em." He pulled her down and kissed her and she blushed, but then the old heat started in her again and she relaxed into his warmth and kissed him back. She looked up dazedly and saw Dr. Banks across the street, coming down his walk. He waved, and she blushed even harder, but Linc just waved back.

"What is this?" she asked, and he said, "This is the new Linc."

"Hey." She tried to push him away. "I like the old Linc. Leave him alone."

"He didn't have enough color in his life. When's Chickie moving in?"

"She's not. She got a lawyer. Crawford's moving out. She's happier than I've ever seen her."

"Good." Linc nuzzled her hair. "Your hair smells so good. What do you put on it?"

"Shampoo. You look great in this sweater. Whose car is that?"

"Ours."

Daisy jerked her head up. "That's ours?"

Linc grinned. "Well, it's ours for a test drive. If we

like it, it's ours forever, and we won't get stuck in the snow anymore."

Daisy stood to see it better. "Can we drive it around and wave at people? I've never had a new car before."

"Later." Linc tugged her down into his lap. "First I have to tell you a story."

"Really?" She snuggled into his arms. "Am I too heavy for your lap?"

"No. Pay attention." She was so warm, he held her close for a moment and couldn't speak. Then she looked up at him, and he began.

"Once upon a time there was a prince who was imprisoned in a tower with track lighting."

"Oh, a *true* story."

"Shut up. Then along came a curly-haired witch and set him free. But he wasn't very happy about it because the witch made him nervous."

Daisy scowled at him, and he remembered the first time he'd seen her, in that horrible hat, and he laughed.

"Why did she make him nervous?" Daisy demanded.

"Because she was a witch. In fact, he was so nervous about her being a witch that he kept trying to change her into a princess."

"Dumbbell," Daisy said, and Linc said, "Exactly.

And he couldn't leave her because they'd made a deal. A Cinderella deal. He had to stay with her until midnight, no matter how weird she acted."

Daisy stuck her nose in the air. "Must have been embarrassing for the prince."

"What he minded most was that she kept interrupting his story."

"Sorry."

"Then one day the witch turned herself into a princess. She dressed in black and sat quietly and behaved herself. She also stopped telling stories." He hugged her tighter at the thought. "It scared the prince into fits because by then he'd fallen in love with her."

Daisy put her face close to his. "Why?"

He grinned and kissed her nose. "Because she was kind and funny and warm and great in bed. She was damn near impossible to tell stories to, though."

"Well, it's a long story."

"We're almost at the end. So the prince told the princess to change back into a witch, and she did, but they had some more problems because witches and princes are going to run into problems no matter how much they love each other."

Daisy got very still in his arms, and he held her close.

"Some more problems?" she asked quietly.

"The kids brought us a record. We'll play it later. Where was I? Oh, yeah. The prince, who was not a complete idiot although he acted like one sometimes, noticed that she wasn't completely a witch, that she had changed a little bit, maybe for him. And so he decided he could change too. So he bought a red sweater even though he really hated it, and he promised her that if she stayed with him he would never again buy track lighting as long as they both lived. And then he waited for her answer. Oh, and he got her a present." He tipped her to one side of his lap, and she clung to him until he'd pulled a ring box from his pocket. "I'm not sure about this," he told her. "I had to guess."

Daisy wanted to tell him that she didn't need a present, that it was all right, but he was looking at her with such concentration that she couldn't. She opened the box. Inside was a chased silver band with freshwater pearls, not the one she'd liked in Pennsylvania, but close.

"It looked like a Daisy Flattery ring," Linc told her. "I thought you might like it better than the old daisy ring."

Daisy sat frozen, trying to absorb what he'd done. He must have gone back over every moment they'd had together to remember this; he must have rethought every minute they'd been together. He was giving her a chance to be Daisy Flattery again.

She held out her right hand. "I want them both."

He held her tightly for a moment, and then he took the ring from the box and slipped it on her right ring finger. "Stay with me, Daisy. Make midnight stay away forever and live with me and have babies with me and adopt some more defective animals with me, and live happily ever after with me."

"I love you," Daisy whispered. "I couldn't possibly ever leave you."

He kissed her then, and she curled into him, holding him close in the bright spring sun, feeling so safe and loved and warm in his arms that she didn't care who saw or what they thought.

"Actually," Linc said into her neck, "for the complete experience of what happily-ever-after feels like, we have to go inside. The neighbors have taken just about all the public happily-ever-after they can stand without calling the police."

Much later, Daisy moved against him drowsily, just enough to wake him up. "I forgot to ask. Does that car come with air bags?"

"Probably," Linc said sleepily into her hair. "Why are you thinking of air bags now?"

"Make a note to ask the dealer." Daisy snuggled closer to him and smiled up at him with such megawatt contentment that she took his breath away. "I want to keep us as safe as possible. I want all the happily-ever-after I can get."

Looking for more classic romance from bestselling author Jennifer Crusie? Then don't miss...

Trust Me on This

By

JENNIFER CRUSIE

Coming from Bantam in December 2010

Dennie Banks is a serious reporter hot on a story, not a con man's moll. Alec Prentice is a clever undercover agent, not a dumb male chauvinist hunk. Dennie and Alec can't quite read each other because they have ulterior motives. Thank goodness their hormones keep getting in the way. Eventually they are going to get to know each other, whether they want to or not.